LOST IN PARADISE

RACHEL LACEY

COPYRIGHT

1

Nicole Morella rested a hand on the doorway as the floor shifted beneath her feet. It had been eight hours since they set sail from Naples in southern Italy, and she hadn't found her sea legs yet. Was it called setting sail on a modern-day, engine-powered boat? Nicole steadied herself as she took in the lounge before her. Couples and groups lingered over drinks at the various tables and sofas filling the room. Laughter and conversation drifted on the air, undercut by gentle strains of jazz music.

Her gaze wandered to the bar, which was just as crowded. A man sat alone at the near end, watching her as he sipped from his drink. She looked away, determined not to lose her nerve and retreat to her cabin on her first night at sea. This trip was her post-divorce gift to herself, and she was going to make the most of it. Tonight, she was going to enjoy a drink at the bar—alone—and she was going to have fun doing it.

About halfway down the bar, a blonde in a red dress sat talking to the man beside her. The seat to her right was empty, and Nicole decided to take it. She crossed the room and slid onto the empty stool, setting her black clutch on the polished wood in front of her. Keeping her back angled slightly toward the man on her other side, who had already begun to eye her with curiosity, she held the bartender's gaze as he sidled over. "Do you have a house red?"

"Yes, ma'am. It's a cabernet blend from Veneto. Very smooth. Would you like to try it?"

"If you like red, you should try the Petit Verdot," a husky British voice said. "It's from Bordeaux, very full-bodied, with just a hint of berries."

Nicole turned to find the woman to her left watching her out of sky-blue eyes as she swirled the contents of her wineglass. "The Petit Verdot?"

"It's excellent." The blonde swiveled to face her, tucking an unruly strand of thick, wavy hair away from her face. She looked to be about Nicole's age—mid-thirties. Light freckles spattered her forehead and chest that, combined with her wild hair and direct stare, lent her a sort of unconventional beauty that Nicole found it difficult to look away from.

"I'll, um, I'll try a glass of that," Nicole told the bartender.

He nodded, moving down the bar to pour her drink.

"American, hm?" the blonde said, still watching her.

Nicole nodded, inexplicably flushed and tongue-twisted when she herself hadn't had even a sip of alcohol yet tonight. She'd booked herself a private Mediterranean cruise to find her footing after the divorce, and she had every intention of doing it alone. Yet, here she was, heart racing for a total stranger. It had been a long time since she'd felt this kind of attraction and even longer since she'd felt it for a woman. "I'm from New York. And you?"

The blonde swirled her wineglass again before taking a

sip. "I live just outside Nice, along the southern coast of France."

"Oh, I thought you were..." Nicole fumbled, grateful as the bartender interrupted to hand her a glass of wine identical to the one the woman beside her held.

"I'm an expat," the blonde said, tossing an amused glance over her shoulder at Nicole. "Born and raised in London."

"Right." Nicole lifted the glass and took a sip. The wine was rich, spicy but fruity. It tasted expensive. And exotic. A lot like the woman next to her. "It's good."

"Glad you think so," she said.

Nicole couldn't figure why the blonde was still talking to her, why she'd basically turned her back to her date when Nicole sat down. But then again, maybe he wasn't her date at all, because he was sitting there now, looking annoyed but also interested, his gaze flicking between the blonde and Nicole. Maybe he was just a random guy hitting on a single woman in a bar, and that woman was now giving him the cold shoulder.

Nicole found her spirits buoyed at the good fortune to have sat next to another single woman...for casual conversation purposes, anyway, not because she was ridiculously attracted to her. "I'm Nicole," she said.

"Fiona," the blonde replied. "Are you here alone, Nicole?"

She nodded. "You?"

"Unfortunately, yes." Fiona dropped her gaze to her wineglass, and Nicole couldn't help admiring the swell of her breasts beneath the formfitting bodice of her dress. Every inch of her was foreign and beautiful, dangerous for a woman committed to a week of solo soul-searching. "I was supposed to meet someone on the boat...a man."

"Oh." Nicole went for casual and hoped she succeeded. It was a good thing if Fiona was straight. It meant Nicole could sit and chat with her harmlessly. Safe.

"He stood me up," Fiona continued, a sharp bite to her tone. "The bastard."

"Aren't they all?" Nicole mumbled, reaching for her wine.

"Indeed," Fiona agreed. "I thought this one was an exception, at least good for a week of sex on the high seas."

The man on the other side of her choked on his drink, and Fiona cast a disapproving glance in his direction at his blatant eavesdropping. Nicole swallowed her laugh with another sip of the luxuriously rich wine Fiona had recommended. So much better than the house red she would have gotten otherwise.

"It's why I generally prefer women to men," Fiona said, a bit louder, and her would-be paramour's cheeks darkened before he turned away.

It was Nicole's turn to choke on her drink. She coughed and spluttered as wine burned its way down her esophagus while Fiona gave her a knowing look that said she'd read her interest and—God, was it possible she returned the feeling?

"So that's my sad story," Fiona said, still holding Nicole in her intense stare. "Why are you all alone on this lovely, romantic boat?"

"It's my post-divorce splurge for myself," Nicole said, clearing her throat and wishing she had a cup of water to cool the burning sensation from inhaling her wine. "I came here to rediscover my sense of adventure or find myself... something like that."

Fiona's eyes crinkled in a warm smile. "I must say I

prefer your story to mine. Not the divorce, but making your own adventure. I like that."

"Thanks." Her cheeks were burning. They were probably as red as Fiona's dress. She really needed to get a grip. Her fingers tightened around the stem of her wineglass. "I'd always wanted to visit the Mediterranean—my family's from Italy originally—and I'd always wanted to take a cruise. So, here I am."

"Ballsy of you," Fiona said, her gaze sliding to the simple gray knit dress that Nicole wore.

She crossed her legs involuntarily. "Do you know this area pretty well, then?"

"I do. It's lovely," Fiona said, tossing her hair over her shoulder as she returned her attention to the wineglass in front of her, leaving Nicole feeling somewhat bereft after the intensity and heat of her gaze. "Although I prefer the French Riviera to Italy or Greece."

"Is that why you moved there?"

"Mm. My favorite place in the world."

"I was in Paris once, for business," Nicole said, remembering that she'd been somewhat lonely and off-balance on that trip too. That was two years ago, when she'd first begun to realize how unhappy she'd become in her marriage. If only she'd known then just how much worse things would get.

"Paris is charming, but if you really want to get the flavor of France, you've got to visit the countryside," Fiona said, swirling her wine.

"I'll have to visit sometime." Nicole felt a tingle in the pit of her stomach, as if she'd somehow accepted an invitation to visit her, when in reality, Fiona was just making idle conversation. Likely, the attraction was entirely one-sided. After all, it had been an eternity since Nicole had flirted with anyone, gone on a date, done anything but steel herself for another battle of the wills with Brandon. She wasn't sure she even remembered how to flirt at this point...

"And what is it that you do for work?" Fiona asked.

"I'm the senior marketing manager for an investment firm in Manhattan."

"Sounds very...corporate."

"It is." Nicole released a sigh that seemed to reach all the way to her soul. "I've been so caught up in work, I'm embarrassed to tell you how long it's been since I took a vacation."

"I'd say you needed this one, then," Fiona said.

"I did. I really did."

The man on the other side of Fiona was watching them again. She gave him an irritated look before her gaze darted back to Nicole. "Care to go for a walk?"

"Um, sure."

"I could use some air." Fiona stood, reaching for her wineglass and a small white purse that she slung over her shoulder.

Nicole followed, bringing her own wine and her black clutch. Alcohol hadn't improved her seaworthiness, though, and she stumbled as they reached the doorway.

"Careful," Fiona murmured, the "r" lost to the cadence of her accent as her free hand grasped Nicole's elbow. Her fingers were warm, her grip surprisingly strong, and Nicole was almost positive that Fiona lingered several moments longer than was strictly necessary.

Fiona Boone led the way onto the deck, dotted here and there with couples in search of fresh air and darkness to cover their actions. She'd thought this cruise was going to be dreadfully dull after Dimitris stood her up. That was before she met Nicole.

She led Nicole toward the rear of the boat to a quiet spot she'd discovered earlier. The curve of the deck hid them from view, but the protruding hulk of one of the lifeboats kept it from being a popular spot...unless one was looking for a place to hide from prying eyes, and right now, that was exactly what Fiona was going for. She leaned her elbows on the railing, taking in the glittering lights of the Italian coastline in the distance. "Beautiful, isn't it?"

"Yeah." Nicole's voice was softer now, as if hushed by the night.

The ship's engine hummed beneath them, accentuated by the splash of water against the hull. Rhythmic and soothing. Fiona had always loved the sea, although she preferred to enjoy it with her feet on dry land. She dangled the wineglass in her left hand, watching the play of white against black as water sprayed out of the darkness below. "I like places like this...out of the way, private. I'm not much for crowds."

"You seem like you could handle just about anything." Amusement laced Nicole's tone.

"I didn't say I couldn't handle them. I just prefer solitude, that's all."

"And here I had you pegged as a social butterfly."

Fiona turned her head, meeting Nicole's gaze in the near darkness. "Is that how you had me pegged?"

"Among other things." Nicole licked her lips, and they glistened in the moonlight, driving Fiona to distraction.

"Good, because I'm many things."

"Tell me a few of them. What do you do for work?"

"I'm an artist." Fiona watched the lights bobbing on the horizon, twinkling like fallen stars.

"Oh, really? What kind of art? Do you paint?"

"Digital mostly, but yes, I do paint." She slid her gaze to Nicole, who was watching her intently. They stood close enough that Fiona could inch her elbow to the right and bump Nicole's. Could have, but she didn't. Not yet, anyway. "Graphic design pays the bills. I paint mostly for myself, although I sell some locally."

"Landscapes or people?"

"Both." She let her gaze drop from Nicole's face to her body, endless curves highlighted by her formfitting dress. Brown hair, hazel eyes, olive-tinted skin. Earth tones. She'd look so much more vibrant in a mossy-green dress than this gray one. "I could paint you, but I'd use brighter colors."

"Like Jack draws Rose in *Titanic*?" Nicole's voice had dropped an octave or two, into the timbre of Fiona's lusty daydreams.

She scoffed. "Hardly. That's a rubbish movie. The ship sinks, and they all die, even poor Jack because Rose's too selfish to share her bit of wood with him."

"Why, Fiona, are you a romantic at heart?" Nicole asked, shifting subtly closer.

"I can be romantic." She lifted her right hand from the railing and brushed it against the curve of Nicole's waist, lingering for a moment there. An innocent enough gesture if Nicole didn't want this to happen, but Fiona had pretty good radar about these things, and she was confident she hadn't read her wrong. Nicole wanted her as badly as she wanted Nicole.

She sucked in a breath at the contact, her eyes finding Fiona's in the dark. Fiona was fairly sure Nicole's interest had more to do with avoiding memories of her ex-husband than Fiona herself, but she didn't mind. She was only looking for a distraction, someone to pass a lonely night or two with here on the ship. It had been months since she'd had sex, too many months, and she was ridiculously horny, an itch she'd been counting on Dimitris to scratch. But now, she found herself even more excited by the prospect of it being Nicole.

In the distance, another boat motored in their direction, engine rumbling in the night. Fiona reached out, sweeping the dark curtain of Nicole's hair over her shoulder. Her fingers brushed Nicole's neck, and she felt goose bumps rise beneath her touch. Fiona leaned in, her pulse going haywire the closer her lips got to Nicole's. They met in a rush of hot breath, noses bumping as their lips pressed together. Nicole let out a hum of pleasure, her eyes sliding shut as Fiona pressed a light kiss against her cheek before bringing their mouths back into alignment.

This time, Nicole opened to her, and Fiona slipped her tongue into her mouth, tasting the same wine she herself had been drinking. Somehow, it tasted sweeter in the hidden pleasure of Nicole's kiss, heady and lush as the Italian countryside they'd left behind that morning. Fiona slid her free hand to the hollow of Nicole's back, pressing her closer, kissing her deeper, drinking her in, suddenly certain this kiss was a hundred times better than anything she would have shared with Dimitris this week.

"Whoa," Nicole whispered as she lifted her head.

"Is that a good thing?" she asked, feathering a hand through Nicole's hair.

She nodded, her face bobbing in Fiona's vision as a shy smile played around her lips. "Better than good."

"I thought so too." Fiona brushed her fingers over the soft fabric of Nicole's dress, smoothing it over the dip of her waist. "In fact, I'm very glad to have been stood up."

"Is he your boyfriend?" There was something hesitant in Nicole's voice now.

Fiona was a lot of things, but she wasn't a cheat, and she wouldn't have Nicole feeling any guilt over Dimitris. "No. He's my... Even lover is too familiar a term. He's a businessman who travels almost exclusively. Occasionally, maybe once or twice a year, if he's in town and we're both currently unattached, we'll get together for a few nights. It's just sex, and in this case, he was called away on business last minute, so I wound up all alone on this lovely boat."

"That's..." Nicole's brow furrowed. "I was married for so long, I don't have any experience with an arrangement like that."

"It's the only kind of relationship I have experience with," Fiona said, a warning in case Nicole wasn't interested in a night of casual sex.

"Oh," she said quietly.

"Your divorce is recent?" Fiona asked.

"Three months. I'm supposed to be using this trip to figure things out by myself."

Fiona sipped her wine, feeling slightly desperate at the thought of having to let her go. She so rarely experienced such an instant connection with someone, let alone this kind of sizzling chemistry. "Would you like me to leave you to it, then?"

"No," Nicole answered quickly, stepping closer.

Fiona met her gaze. "Good."

The other boat had drawn closer, its engine obnoxiously loud. It seemed like their boat, the *Cyprus Star*, had picked up speed, perhaps trying to put more space between itself and its new neighbor. Fiona wished for a table so she could set down her wine. Nicole was stuck carrying wine in one hand and her clutch in the other, no free hands for touching, and maybe Fiona hadn't planned this little rendezvous as well as she'd thought.

"Do they seem too close to you?" Nicole asked, turning her attention to the approaching boat. It seemed to be heading straight for them.

"Mm," Fiona agreed, annoyed at the interruption.

"Maybe it's the Coast Guard?"

"Could be." But the other boat had drawn close enough now that its outline was visible in the night, and it didn't look like an official vessel. There were no identifying marks she could see, no maritime flag or police lights. Instinctively, she stepped into the shadows, drawing Nicole with her.

The approaching boat drew alongside the *Cyprus Star*, and with a horrible screech, their hulls bumped and rubbed, sending a shudder through the deck beneath her feet.

"Oh my God," Nicole whispered.

Almost immediately, men dressed in black tossed ropes to secure their vessel to the *Cyprus Star*. The engine roared belowdecks, an apparent attempt by the captain to shake free, but it was too late. The marauders threw a ladder that hooked onto the *Cyprus Star*'s railing and began scaling it one after another.

"Fuck," Fiona mumbled. She tossed her wineglass into the seething depths of the Mediterranean, then grabbed Nicole's and sent it after hers. She crouched, drawing Nicole down with her, and they pressed themselves into a darkened recess in the side of the ship.

"What's going on?" Nicole whispered. Her hand, still clutched in Fiona's, shook.

"Shh. I don't know, but I don't think it's anything good."

Men's voices shouted in Greek, too jumbled for Fiona to pick out more than the fact that they'd just been boarded by some kind of maritime pirates, and *fuck*, this was bad. She wrapped her arms around Nicole, who promptly buried her face against Fiona's chest, something she would have appreciated a lot more five minutes ago. Now, her heart was about to burst out of her chest, and she wasn't the least bit aroused.

"Everyone listen to me!" a man shouted, followed by the *pop pop pop* of gunfire, and Fiona recoiled. A shaft of moonlight passed overhead, illuminating her red dress like a beacon in the night.

Nicole's body jerked with each gunshot, tension bouncing through her muscles as she braced for the impact of a bullet. Fiona's arms tightened around her, their bodies curled into each other as they huddled in the dark corner of the deck. Men shouted in several different languages, alternating between English, Italian, and something else Nicole couldn't identify.

"Everyone into the dining room," a harsh voice boomed in a heavy accent over the ship's PA system. "We will search the boat room by room, and you'll be very sorry if we find you attempting to hide. It is much better for you if you come to the dining room on your own." He then began to repeat the message in another language.

Nicole could feel herself trembling like a helpless, cornered animal. This couldn't be happening. She hadn't come halfway around the world to be slaughtered on the high seas. Men. So many men. Would they rape the women first? A whimper tore from her throat.

"Shh," Fiona breathed, pressing Nicole's face against her chest. She smelled good, like lavender and honey. Her heart beat wildly against Nicole's cheek, betraying her calm exterior. Still, she seemed more composed than Nicole, who was about one gasping breath away from leaping into the dark water below and taking her chances with the jellyfish and sharks.

"They said not to try to hide," Nicole whispered.

"They've already cleared the decks. They don't know we're here."

"But..."

"It would be foolish to surrender," Fiona said, her words disappearing into the night. "Besides, I have a plan."

"If they find us hiding, they'll torture us, or kill us, or... or..." Nicole's teeth had begun to chatter.

"I'm not handing myself over voluntarily." There was something steely in Fiona's tone that made Nicole cling to her even more tightly. "You can go if you wish, but I hope you stay with me. I think our chances are better together."

"I don't know." Instinct said Fiona was right, but what if the men found them? How could they really expect to avoid capture?

"Trust me." Fiona squeezed her hand.

"What's your plan?"

"Shh...not yet." Fiona pressed them farther into the shadows.

Eventually, things quieted as the hijackers gathered in the dining room on the deck below, presumably having rounded up all the guests they could find. Nicole heard the occasional muffled shout or scream, but the night around them was otherwise still and undisturbed. God, she hoped Fiona knew what she was doing. The air seemed to have dropped about twenty degrees since they'd come outside, or maybe Nicole was just going into shock. Her whole body shook uncontrollably.

"Stay here," Fiona whispered, disentangling herself from Nicole's grip.

"Where are you going?" Nicole clenched her fists against the urge to hold on to Fiona. The thought of being left here alone was too much.

"Shh," Fiona murmured again, climbing to her feet, her fiery red dress muted in the dull glow of the main deck behind them. As Nicole watched in mute horror, she slid through the shadows toward the lifeboat anchored against the *Cyprus Star*'s hull. In daylight, it had gleamed a bright orange beneath the sun. Now, it was just another hulking shape in the darkness.

Nicole gulped. If Fiona's plan in any way involved that lifeboat...

Fiona toed out of her shoes and tossed them overboard before climbing over the railing, disappearing into the darkness. Holy shit, she was as insane as she was gorgeous, as brave as Nicole was terrified, hiding in the shadows while Fiona orchestrated some sort of ninja-like escape. Was she clinging to the side of the boat like a female James Bond? Had she jumped?

Nicole drew on the last of her own courage and climbed to her feet on knees that wobbled like one of those bobble-headed figures that mounted to the dashboard of your car. She took a hesitant step in the direction Fiona had disappeared before movement caught her eye. Instinctively, she melted back into the safety of the shadows.

There was a flash of red as Fiona came into view, climbing back over the railing, lithe as a cat, her unruly blonde hair trailing behind her like a cape. She darted across the deck to Nicole, gripping her hand in ice-cold fingers. "Come," she whispered.

"I can't do...whatever you just did," Nicole breathed. "My arms aren't that strong."

"We're going to hide in the lifeboat." Fiona's grip on her hand tightened. "Hurry."

Hide in the lifeboat? What would happen if the men found them there? But Fiona was already dragging her toward the railing, as determined as Nicole was reluctant.

"Give me your shoes and your purse," Fiona whispered.

Nicole obeyed, sliding out of her heels and handing them to Fiona, who bent and tossed everything through the opening in the lifeboat. The top of it was level with the railing, but its entrance looked impossibly small and hard to reach from where they stood. One slip...

Twenty feet below, the Mediterranean churned black and endless.

"Go," Fiona urged. "I'll follow."

"Okay," Nicole agreed, determined to at least sound brave. She wiped her palms against her dress before gripping the railing. It was cold and slick, dampened by the ocean breeze.

"Quickly," Fiona urged, her hand resting on the small of Nicole's back, a gesture of reassurance.

"Fuck it," Nicole mumbled as she hoisted herself up and over the railing. Water glistened beneath her feet, and her stomach pitched. She definitely shouldn't have looked down. Somewhere below, a man shouted and a woman screamed. Her hand slipped, and she clenched every muscle in her body, determined to make herself one with the cold, wet railing. Nicole didn't care if she looked anywhere near as graceful as Fiona had. She just didn't want to die.

Biceps screaming, she lowered herself until her toes brushed the lip of the lifeboat's open hatch. Awkwardly, she transferred her hands one at a time to the lower rung so she could get her legs inside and drop to safety. She landed in a heap, gasping for breath, heart lodged somewhere in her esophagus.

Inside, the lifeboat was pitch-black. It wobbled as she moved away from the entrance to make room for Fiona to follow. She tripped over something hard that turned out to be one of Fiona's shoes, then bent to scoot them out of the way.

A minute later, Fiona swung into view, her legs gleaming pale in the moonlight as her pleated dress hiked to her waist with the effort of her movement. She crouched against the floor, smoothing it into position as she gestured Nicole ahead of her, deeper into the darkened recesses of the lifeboat.

"Wait...I never even thought." Nicole opened her clutch and pulled out her phone. *Duh.* Why hadn't she thought to call for help sooner? But while she'd had cell service and a Wi-Fi signal earlier today, now her screen showed no signal of any kind.

"They've disabled the ship's service connection," Fiona said under her breath. "Smart of them."

"I don't think this is their first time, do you?"

Fiona shook her head. There was a bump and more shouting from below. She crawled back toward the lifeboat's entrance. "They've detached the other boat. I assume that means they've taken control of ours."

"Shit," Nicole mumbled. The inside of the lifeboat was impenetrably dark and foreboding. She almost preferred the corner they'd hidden in above, although this was no doubt safer. She was crouched against what felt like a bench seat with straps she assumed were some sort of harness or seat belt.

"If they become sufficiently distracted, I think we can

escape." Fiona illuminated the screen of her cell phone over a red cord, and Jesus Christ, was she suggesting they launch the lifeboat on their own? That was either genius...or suicide.

"What if they hear us?"

Fiona turned her head, her expression hidden in the dark. "We'll have to be certain they don't. For now, we lie low."

They crawled to the back of the lifeboat and flattened themselves into the foothold, fingers entwined in silent support. Around them, everything was eerily still and quiet, aside from the steady rumble of the ship's engine. The lifeboat swayed with the rhythm of the boat, turning Nicole's stomach. The movement was disorienting in the dark. She bit her lip to quell the nausea.

Gradually, the engine noise increased, and the ship seemed to pick up speed. The lifeboat vibrated beneath them, and she clenched her teeth to keep them from chattering. Fiona's fingers tightened around hers. They lay like that for what felt like hours but might have been only minutes. It was impossible to tell when every frantic beat of her heart seemed to last a lifetime.

Several times, men walked by close enough for them to hear scattered words—although none in a language Nicole could understand. She hardly dared to breathe until they'd walked out of earshot. Eventually, everything fell quiet, and for what felt like an eternity, they heard nothing but the roar of the engine and the occasional clanking of the lifeboat against its moorings.

Nausea had become her constant companion. Her mouth was dry, and she had to pee. Hiding from pirates was a seriously uncomfortable business.

Noiselessly, Fiona sat up next to her, tugging gently at Nicole's fingers. "It's now or never."

FIONA ILLUMINATED the screen of her mobile phone long enough to glance over the directions for launching the lifeboat. She wasn't wearing her contacts, hadn't thought she'd need them to enjoy a drink at the bar. Consequently, the words were a blur, but essentially, she needed to pull the cord dangling over her head to activate the winch that would lower them into the water.

"Won't that be loud?" Nicole asked, leaning over her shoulder.

"It's a risk we have to take."

"Why?" Nicole demanded quietly. "Do you know something you're not telling me?"

"I understood a few phrases from the hijackers," she said, one hand gripping the release cord. "They're going to begin sending ransom requests at dawn. They've had the engines running at full speed for hours now. I have no idea where we are, but I can't see land anymore."

Nicole blew out a breath. "Ransom?"

"There are some rich and important people on this boat, apparently. Now, I don't know about you, but I'm not worth much, so I'd just as soon get the hell out of here."

"I'm not rich," Nicole whispered. "I'm just blowing off some of my divorce settlement."

"And I didn't even pay for my own ticket," Fiona said irritably. They were wasting valuable time arguing about this.

"We can't be the only ones."

"I'm sure we're not. But what do you think they're going to do with those of us who aren't valuable to them?" Fiona asked. "The engine is loud, and we're at the far end of the boat from where they've got everyone gathered. With any luck, we'll be in the water before they realize what's going on. But we've got to go now, while we still have an hour or two of darkness left to cover us."

"What if the sun rises and we're still just floating alongside the boat?"

"This lifeboat has an engine if one of us can work out how to drive it, but the *Cyprus Star* is going so fast, I think it'll leave us behind all on its own."

"An engine?" Nicole glanced around, eyes wide.

"Lifeboats have come a long way since *Titanic*." Fiona smiled in spite of herself. "Ready?"

"Wait. I don't think this thing is meant to be launched while the boat's moving. It may be bumpy." Nicole grabbed one of the harnesses hanging behind them. She sat and fastened it around herself. "You should strap in too."

Fiona leaned in until their faces were only inches apart, then winked. "I've always preferred to live dangerously."

Nicole's mouth fell open, and Fiona wished for enough light to see the blush she was certain Nicole was sporting. Fiona pulled the cord, fingers tingling as adrenaline flooded her veins. *Here goes nothing...*

The winch activated, whining to life with an alarmingly loud whir and clank. The lifeboat lurched, and Fiona gripped the nearest harness to keep herself upright. But with a screech and another clank, the motor ceased, and they were left right where they'd started.

"Fuck," Fiona muttered. Surely, a luxury vessel like this one was required to test their safety equipment frequently, so chances of mechanical failure were slim. That left the more likely possibility she'd done something wrong.

A dim glow came from Nicole's direction, and Fiona

turned to find her reading the safety manual under the illumination of her phone. "Did you remove the safety pins first?"

"What?" Fiona planted her fists on her hips. They'd made quite a bit of noise now and hadn't moved even an inch toward safety. If one of the kidnappers came to investigate...

"It says there are two safety pins anchoring the lifeboat to the ship. We have to pull them before it can be lowered into the water. See?"

Fiona leaned over to examine the diagram Nicole was pointing at. The safety pins were bright red and probably quite obvious in daylight. In the dead of night, though, it posed a new set of problems. "I'll do it. You stay here."

"I...well..." Nicole looked like she wanted to argue, then changed her mind. "You're more surefooted than I am on the railing. I'll find a way to make it up to you if we survive this."

"I can think of a few ways." Fiona snapped a photo of the diagram with her phone before shoving it down the front of her dress.

"Oh my God." Nicole sounded equal parts incredulous and embarrassed.

"Sorry. I make inappropriate jokes when I'm nervous." But she'd been thinking about sex pretty much since she met Nicole, so she wasn't entirely sure nerves had anything to do with it. Rather than think too much about *that*, she swung out of the boat and gripped the railing.

Don't look down.

She kept her eyes straight ahead as she scaled the railing, wishing her dress didn't have such a long, full skirt. It looked good on the dance floor, showed off her legs when she spun, but right now, it was a serious pain in the ass. She dropped to the deck in an ungraceful heap, her legs shackled by the skirt, which had twisted around her as she climbed.

Sorting herself out, she rose, glancing around to make sure no one was coming. Luckily, it didn't seem like anyone could hear them, now that they'd all gathered in the dining room at the other end of the boat. She slid the phone out of her top and turned on the flashlight, using it to illuminate the metal scaffolding holding the lifeboat to the hull of the *Cyprus Star*.

Surely, anyone on this boat was better suited for this job than Fiona, and yet, here she was, yanking on a red metal pin so she could launch herself and Nicole into the Mediterranean Sea. If they made it that far, they'd worry about the whole "lost at sea" bit later.

The first pin was easy to locate and came right out when she pulled. The second one required a quick consult with the diagram on her phone, but once she'd found it, it too came right out when she gave it a yank. Okay, then. She put her phone away and hauled herself back over the railing, wincing as something sharp bit into her leg. It burned as she reached with her toes for the entrance to the lifeboat. There it was. Almost there.

She eased herself down, and *shit*. Her right foot slid out from under her, wrenching her hands from the railing, and she was airborne. For a moment, she pinwheeled her arms, suspended in time, stomach in her throat as she braced herself to tumble backward into the churning depths of the sea, but then warm hands were around her waist, yanking her to safety. She and Nicole tumbled onto the floor of the lifeboat and lay there, gasping for air.

Fiona's stomach whirled, her entire body prickling with

pins and needles from the close call. "Thank you," she managed finally.

In response, Nicole's arms tightened around her. Her chest heaved against Fiona's, and she realized Nicole was crying. She sat up, swiping a hand beneath her eyes.

Fiona dragged herself to her elbows, disentangling herself from the welcome warmth of Nicole's body. Her right shin stung as it bumped against the seat. "Ouch."

Nicole leaned down, illuminating them with her phone screen. "Holy shit. You're bleeding. Like...*really* bleeding."

Fiona glanced at the blood coursing down her leg. "That must be why I slipped. I didn't even feel it until now. Okay, let's get out of here."

"But your leg..."

"I'll worry about it once we're free of the ship."

"Buckle in," Nicole called as Fiona stood, looping one arm through a harness, and yanked the release cord. This time when the motor whined to life, the crane swung them out over the sea, lowering them into the darkness below. The lifeboat twisted dangerously in the wind. They hit the water with a bone-rattling jolt that knocked Fiona to the floor.

The lifeboat pitched this way and that, careening wildly alongside the *Cyprus Star*, still held tightly to the ship by its moorings. Water poured through the open hatch, soaking them with its icy spray. Fiona struggled to her knees, only to be knocked flat again by the next wave, her body buffeted between the base of the seats and the supply case in the center of the boat.

"Pull the hook release!" she yelled, feeling like an idiot for not strapping herself in as Nicole had done. "The red lever on the control panel."

Nicole reached forward and pulled the lever. For a moment, nothing happened. Then, with a crunch and a clang, the lifeboat lurched free. It slammed into the *Cyprus Star*'s hull and tipped onto its side. Water rushed in through the rear hatch they'd stupidly left open, pouring over Fiona in a soaking wave. She reached out blindly for Nicole's hands but felt only cold metal and colder water. Her head slammed into something hard, and she pressed her lips together, willing herself not to lose consciousness before she'd gotten her head above water.

Lungs burning, she groped for her harness, for air, for Nicole, for anything at all...

3

"Fiona!" Nicole shouted as the lifeboat spun endlessly in the ship's wake. Water washed over her legs, swirling through the darkness. She couldn't see Fiona, couldn't hear her, and was terrified that she'd been swept out the open hatch into the sea. After a disorienting minute, the lifeboat righted itself, and everything went quiet as the *Cyprus Star* left them behind. The lifeboat listed a bit to the side, probably from the foot or so of water that had poured in during their botched launch.

"Fiona," Nicole called again as she unbuckled herself, panic gripping her throat in its icy hand.

"Here," came her raspy voice from the other side of the lifeboat.

"Thank God," she whispered, crawling toward her, feeling her way like a blind woman. "Are you okay?"

"I've been better." There was something cautious—controlled—in her tone that struck fresh fear into Nicole's heart. Fiona sounded strange, and that couldn't be good.

Nicole's hands encountered wet fabric, and beneath it,

cold, wet skin. She found Fiona's hands and gave them a squeeze. "Are you hurt?"

"Just bumps and bruises," Fiona said, quieter now that they were next to each other. "If you say I told you so, I'll kill you."

Nicole choked on a laugh. "The thought never crossed my mind."

"Are we still taking on water?"

"I don't think so. All of this came in through the hatch. I don't think you're supposed to launch at full speed like that, and you're definitely supposed to close the hatch first." Her hands roamed up Fiona's arms, feeling for anything obviously amiss.

Fiona's hands snapped to her wrists, bringing them to her lap. "I'm fine."

"You don't sound fine, and I can't see a damn thing in here. You're scaring me."

"I feel a bit like I've been through a blender, and I'm soaking wet, but I'm okay. Really."

Nicole slid onto the seat beside her and wrapped her arms around her. Fiona was indeed sopping wet and shaking slightly. She must have been tossed completely underwater when the lifeboat tipped over. Nicole could only hope she was telling the truth about her injuries. "What about your leg?"

"If it's still bleeding, I can't feel it."

"I'm serious," Nicole said, resisting the urge to shake her. "If you die, you'll leave me all alone in the middle of the goddamn ocean."

"Need me around to save your ass, hm?" Fiona quipped, a bit of her earlier spunk returning to her voice.

"And, you know, for company." She gave Fiona a gentle nudge. "I'm going to take a look outside and make sure they haven't turned the *Cyprus Star* around to come after us or anything."

Fiona made a sound of agreement, but the fact that she didn't offer to get up herself only reinforced Nicole's worry about her condition.

She felt her way to the hatch and leaned out. The night around them was still and black, gentle waves glistening in the moonlight as they lapped at the boat. "I can see the *Cyprus Star*, but it looks pretty far away."

"That's good news," Fiona said quietly.

Nicole tightened her grip on the side of the lifeboat, leaning farther out. She watched in silence for a few minutes until she could be certain that the *Cyprus Star* was getting smaller, not larger. "It's moving away from us. I think we're in the clear."

She left the hatch, sliding her hands down the row of seats until she found Fiona. She sat, shivering against the chill of the night air.

Fiona rested her head on Nicole's shoulder. "What now?"

"You said there's a motor on this thing, right?"

"Yes, but it's probably wet now, I suppose."

"I have no idea," Nicole said.

"The sun will be up soon. Maybe we should wait until we have some light before we do anything else."

Nicole nodded, her cheek pressed against the top of Fiona's head. "We need to bail all this water out, and I'm sure there's something in here to do it with, but we'll never find it in the dark. My phone's battery is almost dead, so I want to save it in case we come into a signal."

"Fuck." Fiona's head lurched up, narrowly missing Nicole's jaw. "My phone."

With a sinking feeling, Nicole remembered the way

Fiona had stuffed it down the front of her dress before she climbed out to release the safety pins. "Yours is soaked, isn't it?"

"Almost certainly." She moved around beside Nicole. "I can't find it. It's probably floating around in the bottom of the boat somewhere."

"Well, while you were pulling the safety pins, I put both our purses inside the storage chest. Hopefully, it's watertight and the rest of our stuff is okay."

"That was good thinking," Fiona murmured, her head again falling against Nicole's shoulder.

"Together, we make a pretty good team."

Fiona hummed in agreement. They lapsed into silence then, holding on to each other as the lifeboat rocked and swayed to the rhythm of the ocean. Nicole shivered endlessly. She was freezing, and her body ached from various bumps and bruises. Nausea roiled in her stomach from the movement of the lifeboat, and she still had to pee. Her only comfort was the feel of Fiona's body warm and alive next to her.

Sleep was the furthest thing from her mind, but the next thing she knew, Fiona stirred beside her, and her eyes snapped open. Pale light filtered through the interior of the lifeboat, allowing her to get her first real look at it. Having crawled inside in the dark, it was jarring now to see herself sitting in this weird plastic-looking room.

The interior of the lifeboat looked almost like what she imagined a compartment inside a submarine would be like. The outer wall had a long, continuous seat lined with black harnesses for passengers to wear. The middle of the boat was taken up with a big storage compartment that hopefully contained lots of survival equipment. There was a seat behind them that faced a steering wheel and several other controls. Their feet were still submerged in water, and in fact, Nicole couldn't feel her feet. They seemed to have gone numb from the cold.

"Fuck me," Fiona mumbled, rising on unsteady legs.

"Be careful." Nicole stood too, gripping one of the harnesses to keep herself upright.

Fiona ignored her, sliding one hand along the wall as she made her way to the open hatch. She sat beside it, leaning her upper body out into the morning light. "Water, and nothing but water."

"No land?" Nicole felt a sinking sensation in the pit of her stomach, settling heavily against the nausea that had plagued her since they'd boarded the lifeboat.

Fiona looked over her shoulder at her. "Remember how the kidnappers had the engines going full speed all night? I think they were taking us as far out to sea as possible. Easier to keep hostages that way, right?"

"Shit," Nicole murmured.

"We could see the coastline when they boarded, but we lost sight of it almost as soon as they took control of the boat. God only knows where we are now."

Nicole blew out a breath, wishing she didn't feel like she was about to puke. "Well, I mean, the Mediterranean isn't *that* big, is it?"

Fiona arched a brow. "Big enough."

"Right." She sucked in another big breath and blew it out, pressing a hand against her stomach. "First things first, we need to bail out this water, and I need to check you over now that we have enough light for me to see your injuries."

Fiona's expression immediately hardened. "I told you, I'm fine."

"And I saw the blood pouring down your leg last night. You're still standing, so obviously you're not bleeding to death, but you at least need a damn Band-Aid!" Nicole's voice rose. She felt like crap. She was cold and scared, and this was no time for Fiona's foolish pride.

Fiona's chin went up, her jaw flexing for a fight, before she tucked it and acquiesced. "Fine."

"Okay, then." Nicole unlatched and pulled open the supply chest in front of her. She and Fiona busied themselves sorting through its contents, plus the storage bins beneath the seats. The lifeboat, as it turned out, was designed to hold eighteen people. It had food and water rations for that many passengers, plus protective gear that looked like metallic sleeping bags they could zip up in to keep warm.

In even better news, they found a large plastic scoop to bail out the boat, fishing tackle, a first aid kit, a heavy-duty flashlight, and various other survival supplies. And their purses had stayed dry. As Nicole continued to inventory their supplies, Fiona sat by the open hatch and began bailing them out.

"This is going to take a while," she commented without a hint of complaint in her voice.

"We'll take turns. Do you think we can start the motor now?"

"We can try," Fiona said with a shrug.

"The only thing this damn boat doesn't have is a bathroom," Nicole grumbled.

Fiona held up the plastic scoop with a wry smile. "I was thinking about that too. Best I can come up with, we use this and pour it overboard."

Nicole scrunched her face. "That sounds...awkward."

Fiona's eyebrows crawled up her forehead. "Unless you'd rather hang your bare ass out of the boat and hope for the best?"

"Um, not really."

"I'll be the guinea pig, if you like."

"Fine." But discussing their options had only made her more aware of just how uncomfortable she was. She'd had to pee for hours...the whole night, really. She resisted the urge to squirm like a child who's waited too long to ask someone to take them to the bathroom.

"Privacy, please?" Fiona said sweetly, already reaching under her dress to remove her underwear.

Nicole turned and made her way to the back of the lifeboat. She hummed slightly to herself to keep from listening to whatever Fiona was doing behind her.

Finally, Fiona called out. "All finished. It's easier than you think."

"Good." She was too desperate to complain at this point, so she walked to the hatch and took the plastic scoop Fiona held toward her.

"I rinsed it in the ocean, don't worry," Fiona said with a half smile as she turned her back to give Nicole privacy.

She squirmed out of her panties and took care of business as quickly as possible, and sweet Jesus, she felt so much better, it was almost laughable. "Well, that's a relief," she said after she'd leaned out of the boat to rinse their bailing scoop, careful not to drop it.

"There are seasick pills in here," Fiona said, her head popping up from behind the supply chest. "Did you see?"

"I could really use one of those, actually."

"Thought you looked a bit green." Fiona handed her a tablet and a silver water pack.

Nicole took it, twisted open the cap to the water, and swallowed the pill. Then she sat down and leaned her head back, waiting for the churning in her gut to settle. After a few minutes, it really did get better, or maybe that was just wishful thinking. "I feel a hundred percent better than I did ten minutes ago."

"Good," Fiona said, sitting beside her. "I don't want you to die and leave me to fend for myself all alone out here."

"Hey." Nicole took the jab with a smile. "I guess I kinda like you for more than just your ability to help me survive this ordeal, anyway."

Fiona laughed, the first real laugh Nicole had ever heard from her. "Well, that's good to hear."

"Okay." Nicole turned toward her, grabbing the first aid kit off the seat. "Let me have a look at you."

Fiona snatched the case from her hands. "I'm perfectly capable of patching myself up if anything needs patching."

Nicole saw the defensiveness in her eyes, the way her shoulders had hunched beneath the straps of her red dress. Damn, but Fiona really had a hard time accepting any kind of caretaking. Nicole leaned in, pressing a gentle kiss to her cheek as she slid the case from her fingers. "You could, but you don't have to, because you have me. I'm no doctor, but I have two younger brothers. I've patched my share of skinned knees."

"Fine, then," Fiona said, shoulders slumping. "Make it quick, would you? We need to get back to bailing so we can try to get the engine started."

"I'll be quick." Nicole kissed the corner of her mouth, loving the way Fiona visibly softened every time she touched her.

"Not playing fair," Fiona whispered, closing her eyes.

"I never promised to." She gave her another quick peck before turning her attention to the business at hand. She knelt in the cold water that swirled around their feet, lifting Fiona's sodden skirt to reveal a red gash below her right knee. "This looks pretty deep, Fi."

"Mm," was her only response.

"You probably needed stitches, but it's too late for that now, even if we had a way to get you to a hospital. There are some adhesive strips in here. I'm going to use a couple of them to hold it together after I clean it."

"Get on with it, then."

Nicole grinned at the false bravado in her voice. "I really love your accent. Did I tell you that last night?"

"No, you didn't." Fiona's tone softened again, the ghost of a smile on her lips.

"Well, I do." She ripped open an antiseptic wipe and swabbed the wound with it. Fiona hissed out a breath, pressing a hand over her eyes. "Sorry," Nicole whispered, reaching for one of the adhesive strips.

"Want me to talk dirty to you?" Fiona managed a teasing tone despite the pain, choosing to keep the conversation on her accent rather than her injury.

"Later," Nicole said, giving her uninjured knee a squeeze. She placed three strips along the cut and sat back on her heels, satisfied with her work. "Okay, where else are you hurt, or are you going to make me do a full body search?"

Fiona narrowed her eyes at her, leaning forward so that her cleavage was inches from Nicole's face. "I can think of a few body parts I'd like you to search."

"You're impossible," Nicole said, grinning at her. After hours of endless fear and stress, it felt good to laugh, to banter and flirt, to do something *normal*. Even though they still faced an uncertain future, the immediate danger had passed, and Nicole was feeling downright euphoric.

Fiona's lips curved in a soft smile.

"Seriously, is there anything else I should know about, or am I going to have to strip-search you?" Nicole rose on her knees, leaning in so that her hands bracketed Fiona's waist.

Her breath hitched, breasts spilling over the bodice of her dress as she leaned toward Nicole. "Later, when we've got our feet on dry land."

Nicole's heart was beating so hard, she could barely breathe. Heat flooded her body, sweeping past the numbing cold from the water sloshing around her. She closed the distance between them, crawling forward so that her hips met Fiona's, letting the heat between them provide a needed distraction as she ran her hands up and down Fiona's arms, feeling for bumps and wounds as much as she was thrilling herself with the freedom to touch her.

Fiona sucked her bottom lip between her teeth, chest heaving, blue eyes locked on Nicole's. "I know what you're doing."

"I'm giving you the PG version of that strip search." Nicole almost didn't recognize her own voice, it had gone so soft and breathless. Fiona watched quietly as Nicole inspected a bruise by her elbow before running her hands down her sides, squeezing here and there to check for injuries.

"Tease," she whispered, but Nicole supposed since she didn't wince or draw away that none of her ribs were broken.

"You left me no choice." Nicole slid her skirt farther up her thighs, revealing an enormous black bruise. "Shit."

Fiona clamped her thighs around Nicole's hips. "Kiss it and make it better?" she murmured, drawing out each syllable in a way that accentuated her accent, which was certainly not an accident. She was trying to distract Nicole, and she was doing a damn good job of it, because Nicole was so turned on, she could hardly concentrate on the task at hand. And since the sight of the bruise had tears swimming in her eyes as she imagined how badly it must hurt, she bent her head and kissed it.

Fiona arched her back, one hand in Nicole's hair as if she might pull her in for a kiss. Here they were, adrift somewhere in the Mediterranean Sea, Nicole crouched between Fiona's thighs, lips against her skin...as water lapped around them in their not-yet-bailed-out lifeboat. She looked up at Fiona, and for a long moment, neither of them said a word.

Nicole pressed one last kiss against Fiona's thigh before pulling her dress back into place. "Did I miss anything?"

"My head," Fiona said softly, reaching up to touch a spot on the back of her head. "I hit it when I fell. It's just a goose egg, nothing serious."

"There are painkillers in the kit if you want one." Nicole held up a packet.

Fiona crossed her arms over her chest and leveled a severe look at her. "What did I tell you?"

Nicole raised her hands in surrender. "You're fine. Got it." She rose, picked up her purse, and sat beside Fiona, intensely relieved that she didn't appear to be hiding any serious injuries, although the wound on her leg was worrisome. If it got infected, they might be in real trouble.

Fiona watched quietly as Nicole powered on her cell phone to check for a signal. Nothing. And her battery was down to nine percent. She turned it off. Fighting past her disappointment, Nicole opened her purse. "I guess we should take inventory of our stuff?"

Fiona nodded, reaching for her own purse. "Lip gloss, comb, credit card, passport. Not much, I'm afraid."

"I've got breath mints, tissues, cash, credit cards, more lip gloss, and, um, a tampon."

Fiona looked at her. "We might have to get creative if you only have one."

"Oh, I don't... I had my period last week. I just like to be prepared."

"Well, hopefully we'll be home before it's a problem for either of us, then." Fiona held up a sleeve of condoms with a wry smile. "Definitely won't need these."

Nicole grinned. They both leaned forward to put their purses back into the storage box, foreheads bumping in the process. Fiona's gaze dropped pointedly to Nicole's mouth, the tip of her tongue darting out to wet her lips.

Nicole straightened reluctantly. "We really need to get ourselves to dry land so we can think about...other things."

Fiona tossed her one of what Nicole was coming to think of as her signature amused little half grins. "Your turn to bail. I'm going to see if I can sort out this engine."

"Should I really trust an artist to get our engine going?" Nicole teased, seizing the bailing scoop.

"I'd say I got your engine going just fine," Fiona said with a meaningful look. "Besides, I'm the one who got us off the ship, aren't I?"

"Be careful with that leg," Nicole said before she could stop herself, wincing as Fiona bent over the engine, bandages straining at the movement. Several drops of blood beaded around the edges of the wound.

"I am," Fiona said without glancing down at it, her concentration on the engine.

Rather than argue with her—an argument she would surely lose—Nicole sat by the open hatch and began scooping water. She bailed until her right biceps burned before switching to her left arm. The good news was that between her effort and the work Fiona had done earlier, she could see a definite difference in the water level in the boat.

What had been about a foot of standing water had been reduced now to maybe six inches.

Behind her, the engine spluttered, stopped, and then roared to life.

"Holy shit." She turned toward Fiona, who wore a triumphant expression.

The lifeboat lurched beneath them, beginning to move with purpose instead of rolling aimlessly in the waves. Nicole abandoned her task to walk over and stand beside Fiona, who was bent over the controls.

"Which way should we go, do you think?"

"North," Fiona answered without hesitation, pointing at the compass beside the steering wheel. "We were just south of the Italian coastline last night, and the kidnappers must have taken us farther south to bring us out to sea. To keep going south would take us to Tunisia or perhaps Egypt. North should take us back to Italy or Greece, maybe Croatia or Albania, depending on where exactly we are."

Nicole pressed a palm against her forehead. "Wow, you, um, you know a lot more European geography than I do."

"I live here," Fiona said with that look again, the signature look.

"You do. Okay, let's go north. Hopefully, we'll be sleeping in a comfortable hotel bed by nightfall."

"The same hotel bed?" Fiona cocked an eyebrow at her.

Nicole exhaled, meeting her gaze. "Yeah. I'd like that."

4

The engine was still going strong as the sun settled on the horizon to their left. That was a comforting sign that the compass was indeed leading them north, because what the fuck did Fiona know about navigating a boat?

"I think we should bust out the emergency rations," Nicole said from behind her.

"Go for it. Let me know how they taste, because they look disgusting." But she was hungry enough to eat just about anything at this point. At just the thought of food, her stomach growled obnoxiously. Her head hurt, as did her right shin, her thigh, pretty much every part of her that had been pummeled by the boat last night, and she was trying very hard not to take her misery out on Nicole.

Nicole, to her credit, hadn't rubbed her nose in it, other than her little strip search that had left Fiona wet in ways that had nothing to do with the still-soggy dress clinging to her skin.

"It looks like...tofu or something," Nicole said.

"I bet it's not."

"I don't think we want to know what it is."

Fiona glanced over her shoulder, watching as Nicole ripped open the square packet, revealing a substance that did indeed look like a big hunk of tofu, or perhaps cheese. If only it were cheese...

Nicole grimaced as she chewed a bite of it. "It's... I don't even know how to describe it. You'll just have to try it for yourself." She swallowed and reached for her water pack. "But we've got a shit-ton of these things meant for eighteen people, so we might as well keep our strength up. It says they're packed with protein."

"Your face is not selling me on the idea."

"It tastes like...sweet, greasy chalk, but it's food, Fi, and we've got to eat. I've got breath mints in my purse to help with the aftertaste."

Fiona couldn't help the smile that turned her lips at the nickname Nicole had given her. She wasn't the first person to call her Fi. Usually, Fiona didn't like it, but from Nicole, for reasons she'd rather not examine too closely, she did. "Fine. Give me one."

Nicole tossed a packet at her, which she missed like a clumsy idiot, holding in a groan as she bent to pick it up off the floor. At least they'd gotten the boat fully bailed out, but the wet clothes were a problem. She was chilled to the point she might be approaching mild hypothermia and suspected Nicole must be in the same boat.

"What's the plan for the night?" Nicole asked, walking over to peer out of the open hatch as she ate.

"We'll take it in turns, keep the boat pointing north, and hope for the best."

"How much fuel do we have left?"

Fiona squinted at the fuel gauge. "About a third of a tank, I think."

"You think?"

"I'm blind as a fucking bat without my contacts."

"Now you tell me?" Nicole teased, moving to stand beside her. "Shit, you're right. Our fuel is really low."

"Hopefully, land is right over the horizon."

Nicole rubbed her forehead. "What if it's not? What if we run out of fuel?"

"Then we'll float here and eat food cubes until someone finds us."

Nicole looked at her, panic gleaming in her eyes. "What if they don't?"

"They will." Fiona forced certainty into her tone for Nicole's sake. "The Mediterranean is dotted with islands and crawling with boats. It's virtually impossible to get lost out here."

"You're bullshitting me," Nicole said, a smile tugging at her lips. "But thank you."

"It's not entirely bullshit," Fiona said. "Our chances are better here than in the middle of the Atlantic."

"True." Nicole sighed. "I have to admit, I was really looking forward to that hotel room tonight."

"Me too." More than she cared to admit. She ripped open the packet Nicole had given her and took a bite of the crumbly white substance inside. "Jesus Christ, that's awful."

Nicole grinned at her. "It is, right?"

"We need to get dry," Fiona said after she'd managed to swallow her first bite. "We should get out of these clothes and wrap up in those thermal suits before we get hypothermic."

"I think that's smart." Nicole paused. "What do you think's happening on the *Cyprus Star*?"

"Probably best not to think about."

"I can't stop thinking about it," Nicole admitted. "I feel like it's even more motivation to find land, so we can tell the police what we know, maybe help the other passengers get rescued."

"Yes." Fiona hadn't let herself dwell on the plight of the passengers on the *Cyprus Star*, but Nicole was right. They had vital information about the hijacking. "Hopefully soon."

They kept talking as they ate, distracting themselves from the disgusting food and discomfort of their situation, although Fiona's aches and pains had grown impossible to ignore. After they'd finished, Nicole passed out breath mints as promised, as well as thermal suits. And she didn't say a word when Fiona snagged one of the aspirin packets from the first aid kit—not even a raised eyebrow—which, frankly, Fiona really fucking appreciated.

Actually, she appreciated pretty much everything about her. Nicole had been straightforward and resourceful throughout their ordeal, despite her initial panic when the pirates boarded the boat. At this point, Fiona was somewhere between smitten and obsessed, unable to think about anything but fucking her as soon as they made it to dry land, which she really hoped would be soon, because she was so done with this lifeboat and pretty much everything about their situation except Nicole's company.

But the emergency ration curbed her hunger, the aspirin soothed her pain, and the thermal suit—once she'd shed her dress and climbed inside—offered some much-needed warmth. "I'll take the first shift."

"Are you sure?"

Fiona nodded. As exhausted as she was, she was too wired to sleep right now. She needed the quiet reflection of a little time to herself while Nicole slept first.

"This feels so good," Nicole murmured, lying somewhat awkwardly across the row of seats. "Tell me when you're ready for a break."

"I will. You get some sleep," Fiona told her. They'd barely slept last night, and they'd get sloppy if they didn't rest tonight. They couldn't afford to get sloppy.

Something she hadn't voiced out loud yet was her fear that no one was looking for them. No one would have reported them missing. If the kidnappers had even noticed she and Nicole were gone, they would keep that information to themselves, would pretend they still had every passenger to maximize their ransom demand. Until the *Cyprus Star* was rescued, no one would know she and Nicole weren't on it.

It was up to them to save themselves.

Behind her, Nicole's breathing evened out. Apparently, exhaustion left her able to sleep while laid out across a row of plastic seats that couldn't be even remotely comfortable. For a few minutes, Fiona just watched her sleep, admiring the steady rise and fall of her chest and the way her eyelashes occasionally fluttered.

God, she was beautiful, with those impossibly dark lashes and all that smooth, tanned skin. Her hair had been pin straight when they met—no doubt the product of a hairdryer—but now it curled around her face in soft waves and the occasional ringlet, not so unlike Fiona's own unruly corkscrews. She resisted the urge to reach down and twirl one of Nicole's curls between her fingers.

Reluctantly, she returned her attention to the instruments in front of her. The compass showed they were still headed north, although no land dotted the horizon ahead. After a while, her eyelids grew heavy beneath the steady hum of the engine as darkness fell across the sky. She'd been running on adrenaline for twenty-four hours now, and she had just crashed like slamming headfirst into a cement wall.

Determined to give Nicole a proper rest before she caved to her own exhaustion, she resorted to pinching herself periodically to prod herself awake, but eventually, even that wasn't enough. She climbed out of the thermal suit and walked the lifeboat end to end—not giving a flying fuck that she wore only her underwear, because she was lost at sea, so who cared? If only there'd been room for yoga. That might have helped calm the growing restlessness and frustration inside her.

After prowling the boat, she returned to the captain's chair—still wearing only her underwear—and double-checked they were still headed in the right direction. Off to the right, a light glimmered on the horizon. A jolt raced through her system, erasing all symptoms of fatigue. Another boat? Land?

Should she change course and head toward it? What if it was the *Cyprus Star*? She hoped they were miles away from it by now, but for all she knew, they were unknowingly following in its wake. Before she could decide what to do, the light blinked out, snuffed by the horizon.

Maybe it was for the best. If it was another boat, it was surely moving faster than they were. With their fuel running critically low, it would be foolish to start motoring in circles out here, chasing lights on the horizon. Their safest course was to keep heading in a straight line until land came into sight. Hopefully, friendly land, because there were a few countries out here she wasn't wild about crashing into.

Now that the excitement of the light had passed, fatigue swept over her again. How long had it been since Nicole fell asleep? Minutes? An hour? Hours? She had no fucking clue. So she got up and started pacing again, back and forth, back and forth, checking their course on the end of each loop. She hurt, her bones rattled with cold, and her limbs felt like they were made from lead.

Eventually, after what she hoped had been hours and not minutes, she picked up her thermal suit and tapped Nicole on the shoulder.

"Mm," Nicole murmured, rolling toward her.

Fiona braced a hand against her chest to keep her from rolling off the narrow row of seats onto the floor. "Careful," she whispered.

Nicole's eyes popped open, widening as she took in Fiona's mostly naked form in front of her. She cleared her throat, blinked, and dragged her gaze up to Fiona's face. "Did you, um, did you get hot in the suit?"

"No, but being warm made me too sleepy." Fiona stepped into her suit, zipping it up to her chest. It was like a body-shaped, spacesuit-looking sleeping bag, and it was warm, but not as hot as the look in Nicole's eyes when she'd seen Fiona's bare breasts.

"I'm up." Nicole dragged herself upright, rubbing at her eyes. "Your turn to sleep. You look exhausted."

"I am." Too tired to debate the point or even fully appreciate the fact that Nicole had just seen her in her underwear. She lay down in the spot Nicole had vacated, watching the sway of her hair over her shoulders as she sat in the captain's seat until Fiona slipped into unconsciousness.

Nicole's hair brushed against her cheek. They were in bed together, and Fiona wanted to kiss and touch every inch of her, but her arms were trapped against her chest, and her pillow felt like it was made of cement. She groaned in frustration.

"Fi...wake up..." Nicole's voice filtered through her brain, drawing her back toward reality. The first thing she registered was the silence. No sound of the engine rumbling beneath her.

"What...?" she mumbled, scrambling to gather her wits as her eyes blinked open. God, she was so tired, she felt drunk.

"We ran out of gas about an hour ago, but that's not why I woke you," Nicole said. "Listen."

Fiona blinked into the darkness, straining her ears to hear anything other than the hollow slap of water against the hull and her own ragged breathing. Beyond all that, she could just make out a rhythmic roar that almost sounded like...

"Hear that?" Nicole said, excitement in her tone. "Waves crashing! And that means..."

Fiona sat upright, reaching for her in the darkness. "Land."

Nicole clutched Fiona's hands, tears spilling over her cheeks. "We did it. We're safe."

"I hope so," Fiona said, her voice even raspier than usual from sleep. "I don't see any lights. If we were going to wash up on the beach of that fancy hotel we've been dreaming about, there would be lights."

"Dammit, stop being so rational." Nicole leaned forward to fish her cell phone out of the storage chest. Sending up a silent prayer, she powered it on. She and Fiona waited in breathless silence as it searched...and searched...for a signal. "Nothing." And her battery was down to four percent. She turned it off. They'd never found Fiona's phone. Presumably, it was at the bottom of the Mediterranean.

"Maybe the fancy resort is up the beach a little ways," Fiona said.

"It sounds kind of rough out there. What if we're about to crash into rocks or something?"

Fiona's arm snaked around her waist, pulling Nicole onto the seat beside her. "Then we'll go down together, fighting."

"Now you're scaring me." Nicole turned toward her, wrapping her arms around her in the darkness.

Fiona's lips pressed against her neck. "Sorry. I'm not trying to. But to prove I can learn from my mistakes, let's put our harnesses on in case we're about to have another rough landing, hm?"

"Yes." Nicole put her phone away and fumbled with the straps behind her, securing the harness across her chest as Fiona did the same beside her. "If we can float around out here until dawn, we'll be able to guide ourselves in."

"I thought you said we'd run out of fuel?" Fiona rested her head on Nicole's shoulder the way she'd done last night, and Nicole couldn't remember ever feeling closer to another person.

She burrowed her fingers into the silvery fabric of Fiona's thermal suit. "We have, but there are paddles."

"Okay. That's good." Fiona's voice grew softer. "Here's hoping that hotel has room service, because I'm not going to want to leave the bed once we get there."

Nicole bit back a laugh. She knew Fiona was mostly just trying to lighten the mood, but the chemistry between them was real and potent, and that scared Nicole as much as it thrilled her. She'd known she was bisexual since she was a teenager and had a girlfriend briefly in college, but they hadn't done much more than kiss, and Nicole had met Brandon soon after. She'd never had sex with a woman. Something told her that was not the case for Fiona.

But if this disastrous year had taught Nicole anything, it was to grab ahold of the unexpected. If she and Fiona survived this ordeal, they deserved to enjoy themselves afterward. Nicole had thought she needed time alone to figure out who she was and what she wanted out of life, but maybe she'd been wrong. Maybe she needed to explore her sexuality as part of the journey, and maybe Fiona was the perfect person to help her.

Something scraped along the underside of the lifeboat with a hollow grinding sound that had every hair on Nicole's body standing on end.

"We didn't plan this well," Fiona said. "If we're going to get tossed out on our asses, I wish I had my clothes on instead of this ridiculous spacesuit sack."

Nicole swallowed another laugh. "We're going to look so stupid when we wash up on that fancy resort's big sandy beach."

"Ridiculous," Fiona agreed, her arm tightening around Nicole's waist.

"Maybe we should just...take them off..." She gasped as the lifeboat slammed into something with a resounding crunch that rattled her bones. "Oh God."

"Look at that," Fiona said, sounding a bit breathless. "This time I didn't fall on my head like an idiot and almost drown inside the fucking boat."

She'd almost drowned last night? Nicole didn't even have time to process that information before the lifeboat lurched again, tipping dangerously to the side. "Shit."

"Fuck," Fiona said on the same breath.

They clutched each other in the darkness. The lifeboat seemed to have run aground, but it didn't feel like any kind of ground they wanted to be on. Waves crashed against them, tipping their boat precariously back and forth with each push and pull of the ocean.

"Where's the flashlight?" Fiona asked.

"Um. It was up there on the control panel by the compass, but I can't see it now."

"Maybe we should try to have a look around, or maybe we should just sit tight until the sun rises. I'm not sure which."

"Let me see if I can find the flashlight," Nicole said, because she was closer to the controls. She reached over blindly, her hand grazing the steering wheel. Reluctantly, she unbuckled herself so she could reach farther. If their boat was about to tumble into something awful, she'd rather know about it than sit here in the darkness, waiting blindly to drown.

"Be careful," Fiona said from behind her.

"Always." She closed her fingers around the flashlight's heavy metal base, located the power button with her thumb, and pressed. Light flooded the interior of the lifeboat, illuminating the floor, which was still blissfully dry. No sign of any holes or leaks from the rocks they'd scraped over and were currently lodged on.

Blowing out a breath, she aimed the beam out the window over the steering wheel, squinting against the glare off the plexiglass. "It's hard to see anything."

"Land?" Fiona asked.

"Um, I think...I actually think I see a beach, oh my God, I really do!" Her heart leaped at the sight. That pale stuff in the distance sure looked like sand, but why was it so far away?

"Let me see." Fiona was at her side, the suit sagging around her waist, and Nicole was almost too excited about the prospect of dry land to notice her bare breasts. Almost...

"Look." She gestured with the flashlight.

"We're still in the water," Fiona said, her expression puzzled. "We're nowhere near the shoreline."

"What are we stuck on, then?" Nicole asked, trying to ignore the sick feeling in the pit of her stomach that said this wasn't as good as she hoped it might be.

"Rocks?" Fiona suggested. "The reef, perhaps."

"Maybe." Flashlight in hand, Nicole made her way to the other end of the boat, hampered by the sleeping bag that forced her to shuffle.

Fiona chuckled behind her. "I think we need to put our clothes back on. Hopefully, they've dried out some."

"I think that's an excellent idea." She leaned out the hatch, aiming the flashlight's beam left and right. Waves crashed around them, breaking over dark shapes that seemed to stretch endlessly in both directions. "A reef, I think. But I'm not sure."

"Okay. This is not bad news. Let's get dressed. It must be close to sunrise by now, and once we can see, we'll work out how to get the boat free or swim for it if we have to."

Silently, they zipped out of their thermal suits and put on their dresses. Nicole never wanted to wear this stupid dress again. It was cold and damp, clinging to her so that her whole body felt clammy, but it sure beat the thermal suit for mobility, so she'd suck it up.

Fiona's red dress still looked stunning on her, with its snug, low-cut bodice and full, pleated skirt. God, how did she look so beautiful after twenty-four hours in a lifeboat? Her blonde hair was a mess, but the kind of mess that made Nicole want to bury her hands in it and draw her in for a never-ending kiss.

"Don't look at me like that," Fiona said. "We aren't on dry land yet."

"Sorry." She clicked off the flashlight, plunging them into darkness. "But it's seriously not fair for you to look that gorgeous."

"Stop," Fiona muttered, but there was laughter in her tone.

Nicole looked out the open hatch. "The sky's getting lighter over there. It must be almost morning."

"Good. We'll be on shore before you know it."

"I sure hope so." Nicole stared into the swirling darkness. She very much did *not* want to get tossed on those rocks, or coral, or whatever it was. They'd be a bloody mess in no time, and she wasn't at all confident a shiny resort waited just up the beach. She and Fiona sat together by the hatch, hands clasped as they watched the sun rise over the ocean.

"It's beautiful," Fiona murmured.

"It really is."

"Oh." Fiona straightened, leaning forward. "I just saw a dolphin jump."

"No way, really?"

Fiona nodded. "That must be a sign of good luck, right?"

"Must," Nicole agreed, but the lifeboat tipped more precariously with each wave that crashed against it, swaying this way and that until finally, by unspoken mutual agreement, they got back into the seats and harnessed themselves in.

The lifeboat rolled almost horizontal against the reef, and Nicole's stomach rolled with it. She yelped, bracing herself for whatever came next. Fiona's fingers tightened around hers. And then, with a groaning crunch, the boat slid free.

"Holy shit," Nicole breathed.

"Time to dig out those paddles." A smile broke across Fiona's face, even brighter than the sun glistening on the horizon. "Our beach resort awaits."

5

Fiona dug her paddle into the surf, driving them toward shore while Nicole did the same on the other side of the boat. Each wave brought them closer to the sandy beach ahead, before sucking them right back out, and goddammit, she was tired. She would have suggested they ditch the lifeboat and swim for it, but the more she looked at the land ahead, the more she felt they'd landed somewhere uninhabited and might need the supplies onboard the boat—not to mention the boat itself— to survive.

She gritted her teeth against the pull of the surf, digging her paddle into the water. Another big wave lifted them forward, and she did it all again. Finally, arms trembling with fatigue, she felt the belly of the boat scrape sand.

"Bail," she called, jumping out through the hatch. Nicole followed, and together—albeit awkwardly—they pushed and shoved the boat up the beach. Once it was grounded, Fiona fell to her hands and knees in the surf, fighting the ridiculous urge to kiss the sand beneath her feet.

Nicole dropped down beside her, tears on her cheeks. "We did it. We really did it."

"We did." She looked over at Nicole, and then they were in each other's arms, laughing and kissing. She cupped Nicole's face in her hands, smoothing her thumbs over her cheeks as she brought their mouths together. Nicole tasted like salt. Hell, every bit of them tasted like salt at this point, but right now, it was the best thing Fiona had ever tasted. It was the flavor of success, of victory, of life.

"I don't see our hotel," Nicole murmured against her lips.

"Fuck the hotel." Fiona wasn't ready to think about their new reality yet. For this moment, she just wanted to revel in their relative safety and the freedom to kiss this beautiful woman who was currently occupying every free ounce of her brainpower.

"I think—"

She swallowed Nicole's protest with another kiss. "Don't think. Not yet. Just take one minute with me here to enjoy this."

And that did the trick. Nicole's tongue swept into her mouth, and then they were kissing for real, the kind of kiss that flooded Fiona's whole body with warmth and need, that sent her pulse whirling and left her gasping for air. Nicole's hands slid up her back, anchoring them together as the ocean pushed and pulled around them, knocking them into each other until they went down in a tangled heap of limbs and laughter.

Nicole sat up, spitting out a mouthful of ocean water and sand. "Kissing on the beach sounds so much more glamorous than it is."

"We're not exactly in top form." Fiona's head was spinning, and not just from the kiss. She was physically exhausted, sleep-deprived, starving, and probably a bit dehydrated. Not to mention, every inch of her body seemed to throb with pain. A red rivulet ran down her leg, and she adjusted her skirt to hide it. She'd probably knocked off all the adhesive bandages by crawling on her hands and knees in the sand. That hadn't been smart, but she'd completely forgotten about her injury in the heat of the moment.

"What now?" Nicole asked, turning to take in their surroundings.

White sand curved around them in a sort of inlet, giving way to grass and scrub that eventually turned into rock-strewn hills. To their right, a stone outcrop rose high overhead. It was gorgeous. Stunning. And desolate.

"I don't know," Fiona answered honestly. "I don't know if we're on a deserted island or just a stretch of the mainland no one's built on yet. Our resort might be right over that hill. Or...it might not."

"I don't think it is," Nicole said quietly, drawing her knees up under her chin.

"I don't either."

They sat for a moment in silence, just staring at each other. The surf swirled around them, and Fiona wished desperately that she were dry, that she didn't have sand all over her body or blood streaming down her leg or the beginnings of a pounding headache.

"I think we should try to climb that rock," Nicole said finally. "Because civilization really might be on the other side. If it's not, we need to see if we can find shelter, because I don't know about you, but I don't want to spend another moment on that boat. I'll bring my phone up there too and try to get a signal."

"I like your plan," Fiona said, immensely relieved to

have one. "I just need to make a quick wardrobe adjustment before we go rock climbing."

"A wardrobe adjustment?" Nicole raised her eyebrows.

"I'll be right back." She got to her feet and climbed inside the lifeboat. There, she stripped out of her dress before poking through the supply chest until she found the fishing knife. The damn dress was heavy as stones when it was wet. It clung to her legs like a shroud when she walked, and besides, all that extra fabric could come in handy in other ways.

Knife in hand, she hacked away the majority of the skirt, leaving herself enough fabric to reach mid-thigh. She leaned out and rinsed it in the surf to get out as much sand as possible before putting it back on. Then, looking down at the open gash below her knee, she cut a strip from the folds of the skirt and wrapped it around her leg, knotting it in the back. Satisfied, she cut several more lengths of fabric to tie around their feet—because neither of their high-heeled shoes were suitable for hiking of any kind.

Nicole's jaw fell open when Fiona climbed out of the lifeboat. "Well, that's short...sexy...um..."

"Practical for hiking?" Fiona offered.

"Yeah, that's totally what I was thinking too," Nicole said with a grin, her gaze dropping to Fiona's exposed legs. "Shit, your leg."

"You can play doctor again later, if we don't find civilization over the hill. Deal?"

Nicole nodded. "What's the other fabric for?"

"Our feet."

"Oh." She followed Fiona up the beach, where they sat side by side on a large rock.

"This looks like Greece to me," Fiona said as she began

wrapping lengths of fabric around her feet. "There are dozens of small, uninhabited islands like this one."

"We don't know yet that it's uninhabited," Nicole reminded her.

"Right." But her gut told her they weren't going to find civilization over the hill, and Nicole knew it as well as she did. "But even if it is, we're not far from the mainland. Fishermen visit these islands all the time. Someone will come by soon and find us. Or maybe we can see something from the top of that rock that will lead us in the right direction."

Nicole backtracked to the boat to get her phone.

"Give it here," Fiona said. "I have pockets."

Nicole's gaze dropped to Fiona's hips. "That really is the perfect dress...but it's soaking wet. I'll carry my phone."

They clasped hands as they made their way over the scrubby terrain toward the outcropping of rocks. It was hard enough to climb in wet dresses and scraps of fabric wrapped around their feet without also being exhausted and weak from their ordeal at sea. But the change of scenery seemed to have given them both a boost of adrenaline.

They scrambled and climbed until they'd reached the top of the overlook, from which they had a panoramic view of their surroundings. The Mediterranean spread before them in all its turquoise beauty, crashing impressively against the reef they'd been stuck on during the night. Beyond that, Fiona saw nothing but endless sea.

Turning, she surveyed whatever the fuck they'd landed on. The mainland? An island? She still wasn't sure. If it was an island, it was too big to see the far side of it, but the coast curved sharply enough in both directions to make her think it might meet on the other side if she could only see over the rocky, scrubby hills before her.

"No hotel," Nicole said quietly. She sat abruptly on the

rock beneath them as if all the wind had just gone out of her sails.

Fiona knew the feeling. She desperately wanted a hot bath and a soft bed...preferably with Nicole in it. She hadn't realized how much she'd been counting on the possibility of a hotel until it wasn't there.

Nicole powered on her phone, and they watched as it searched in vain for a signal before abruptly shutting off. "Battery's dead," Nicole mumbled.

"It's okay. We'll find that hotel on our own."

"Will we, though?" There was something wild in Nicole's eyes Fiona hadn't seen there before. "What if we're just two people who disappear at sea and are never heard from again? You know those people must think they're going to get rescued too...right until the end."

"Those people are in much more remote places. We're somewhere off the coast of Europe, not way out in the middle of the ocean." The moment clearly called for a pep talk, but they weren't exactly Fiona's forte. It was no accident that she lived alone, worked alone, spent the majority of her life alone.

She thrived in solitude, hated placating other people's emotional needs. And yet, as she stared into Nicole's terror-filled eyes, she found herself reaching deep for the words Nicole needed to hear. "Someone will find us. I really do think so. And if they don't, we'll save ourselves. We've got a boat filled with supplies, and that's a lot more than most castaways have."

She did believe that, but they still might be stranded for days...weeks...longer. The truth was, only years of meditation practice were keeping Fiona's breathing in check right now. Her heart raced, and her skin prickled uncomfortably. She wanted to go home. She needed her rituals and routines and the sense of control they gave her.

Beside her, Nicole sucked in a lungful of air and blew it out with a decisive nod. "You're right. Someone will find us. Let's go build an SOS on the beach to help them out."

At least Fiona's bullshit pep talk had worked for one of them.

Nicole watched the sun set in a daze. She and Fiona had spent the day exploring the area around their little harbor. They'd found some berries they'd been too afraid to eat, built an SOS on the beach, and found a smooth, flat spot on the rock where they'd brought two thermal suits to camp out overnight. Nicole would rather have had a shelter to sleep in, but Fiona had convinced her there were no predators on the island that would eat them while they slept. Indeed, they'd seen nothing all day but seabirds and one small lizard. And so they sat, watching the sun slide beneath the horizon as they ate lifeboat food rations and drank stale, metallic-tinged water.

"Tomorrow, we'll use that fishing tackle in the lifeboat and go fishing," she said.

Fiona made a sound of agreement, her eyes locked on the horizon. She'd been quiet for the last few hours, almost introspective. Nicole couldn't shake the feeling that she wanted to be left alone, wanted to retreat to her real life, whatever that was like. Did she have a studio in her house where she painted all day?

Nicole visualized it with a smile. But Fiona had said she mostly worked in graphic design. She could picture that too. Fiona seated at her computer, hair tied back and perhaps glasses perched on her nose, creating fancy graphics that Nicole herself might use as she branded a new investment portfolio.

"How's your leg?" she asked as her gaze fell on it. She'd cleaned and rebandaged it earlier today, but the wound looked red and swollen around the edges, and she wished she had some antibiotics to give Fiona.

"It'll be fine," Fiona responded without moving.

That wasn't quite the same as her usual answer of *I'm fine*, and the difference bothered Nicole. "We've got plenty of pain pills if you need them."

"Mm," Fiona said, eyes still locked on the sunset.

Nicole watched her for a moment of uncomfortable silence before finally heaving a resigned sigh. "You're freaking me out a little bit."

Fiona turned, her gaze locking onto Nicole's. "What? Why?"

"You're just...not quite here or something."

"Sorry." Fiona stretched out on her sleeping bag, hands clasped over her waist. "I'm not used to spending so much time with someone, I guess. Sometimes, I just don't have anything to say."

Nicole lay beside her on her own bag. "Are you saying I talk too much?"

A soft smile curved Fiona's lips. "No. Only that I don't talk enough. I'm sorry. I'm tired."

"God, me too." They'd barely slept last night or the night before. "We'll feel better in the morning."

"We will." Fiona reached over to take her hand, a gesture that had lent comfort and connection between them since that first night on the *Cyprus Star* as they hid in the shadows behind the lifeboat.

"Good night, Fi."

"G'night," she slurred, her eyes already sliding shut.

Nicole held tight to her hand as she drifted into a deep, dreamless sleep. The next thing she knew, a bird squawked, startling her awake. The sun peeked over the hill to her left, and Fiona's sleeping bag was empty. Disoriented and sluggish, she sat up, rubbing at her eyes. Holy crap. She had apparently slept without stirring from sunset to sunrise.

Her eyes settled on Fiona, a vision in red down on the beach. She sat on a flat rock near the water's edge, hands on her knees as though she were meditating. Maybe that was what she'd needed last night when she got so distant and weird. Was she really so unused to the company of another human being? She'd been planning to spend a week on the *Cyprus Star* with her lover, after all.

Nicole watched as Fiona got to her feet, stretching like a cat before folding herself into some kind of yoga pose that left Nicole with pretty much no choice but to stare at her perfectly shaped ass...and the red satin panties peeking out from beneath her newly short skirt.

Well, she could have turned away, gotten out of bed to go find a place to pee, but no, she just sat there, helpless to do anything but watch Fiona go through her morning yoga routine. Mixed in with her gawking, though, Nicole worried over the scrapes and bruises visible on Fiona's skin and wondered how the wound on her leg was doing this morning.

Finally, Fiona headed in her direction, scaling the rocks like a sea nymph, her lean muscles flexing impressively as she climbed. She arrived at their sleeping bags with a bright smile, the sunrise dancing in her eyes. "Morning, sleepyhead." She tossed a food ration in Nicole's lap and sat beside her with one of her own.

"I've been up for a little while," Nicole said, and some-thing must have shown in her eyes, because Fiona grinned.

"Were you up here watching me?"

Nicole grinned right back at her. "Maybe."

"I hope you enjoyed the show."

"Oh, I did. It was almost as good as a cup of coffee."

Fiona's lips quirked. "You Americans and your coffee."

They busted into their breakfast then, making small talk to distract themselves from the nasty taste of the food cubes. As gross as they were, though, she and Fiona were lucky to have them, and to have the rations for eighteen people. It would keep them going for a long time if necessary.

After they ate, they freshened up and set off down the beach for some exploring. They'd decided to walk as far as they could in one direction to see if they ended up back where they'd started, confirming they were in fact on an island. They would walk until the sun was directly overhead before turning around to make sure they'd return to their campsite before nightfall, scouring the island for fresh water as they walked.

Yesterday, Fiona had cut open several of the thermal suits, separating the shiny outer layer so they could wrap it around their shoulders to protect them from the relentless sun overhead. They each wore a sun cape today as they walked, glistening in the sunshine. It seemed to be working, though. Neither of them had sustained more than a minor sunburn.

"What's that?" Fiona asked suddenly after they'd walked in silence for a while.

Nicole followed her gaze to see a man-made structure about a hundred yards inland. "Holy shit."

"It looks like some sort of ruins."

Actually, it did. Nicole's initial excitement gave way to

disappointment as she realized they were still alone, but hey, at least other humans had lived here at some point in history? They walked toward it together, picking their way over rocks and shrubs.

The structure looked like it had once been a pavilion or a shrine. Its white marble floor was mostly intact, cracked here and there and interspersed with weeds and vines. White columns were in various states of disrepair. A few still stood tall and proud, but most had crumbled to the earth.

"It's beautiful," Fiona muttered, standing with one hand against a column like a Greek goddess, golden curls tumbling over her shoulders, red dress clinging to her slender frame until it met its knife-altered end against her thighs.

"*You're* beautiful," Nicole said. "This place is a crumbling mess."

Fiona looked at her over her shoulder. "It's a piece of history. Maybe no one's stood here for centuries. The way it's fallen is like...art."

"Would you paint it?" Nicole asked. "If you had your stuff with you?"

"I would. And I'd paint you in it."

Nicole shook her head. "I'd take a picture of you standing there, just like that, so you could paint it for me. Now *that* would be art."

Fiona ignored her, walking between the fallen columns, seemingly lost in thought, or maybe just lost in art. Nicole was intrigued by this side of her, these glimpses of a whimsical, aloof artist that seemed so at odds with the confident, forward woman who'd brought Nicole to a secluded corner of the ship to seduce her before launching their escape.

What was Fiona like in real life? This Fiona or that one? Neither? A combination of the two?

"Aphrodite," Nicole said. "She's the goddess of love, right?"

"That's right."

Nicole followed her across the marble floor, her cloth-wrapped feet soundless against its smooth surface. "Imagine if someone showed up here right now, on this beach where no one lives, and found us standing here in this ancient structure like Greek goddesses brought to life."

Fiona turned toward her then, a smile dancing in her eyes. "I'd say we qualify as goddesses for escaping and surviving the way we have."

"Me too."

"Athena," Fiona said, "the goddess of war. Hera, the queen."

"You know a lot about Greek goddesses."

Fiona had stopped walking, and Nicole stood beside her, gazing down at the beach. It looked like one of those graphics on Pinterest, "Top Ten Remote Beaches for a Romantic Getaway," with turquoise waves lapping at the sand, ancient ruins overhead, and rolling hills behind.

"If this really is a deserted island, perhaps we should move our camp here," Fiona said. "It's lovely."

"I agree."

Fiona turned toward her, a hunger gleaming in her blue eyes that had nothing to do with the food ration they'd brought with them to share for lunch. The same hunger had been simmering inside Nicole since she'd first caught sight of Fiona at the bar. It was the reason she'd followed her to that darkened corner of the deck where they'd shared their first kiss. The memory of it sent a thrill through her system.

Fiona leaned in, one hand finding its way into Nicole's hair, much the way she'd done that night on the *Cyprus Star*, and like that time, goose bumps rose on Nicole's skin, a shiver of anticipation. Her lungs expanded, filling with fresh sea air. "Kiss me."

As if she'd been waiting for that invitation, Fiona brought her lips to Nicole's. They met hesitantly at first, as though weighed by the knowledge that there was nothing stopping them this time, no reason not to do this...more... anything they wanted to. Nicole was drunk on the possibilities, somewhere between thrilled and terrified.

She settled her hands on Fiona's waist, loving the womanly shape of her, the dip and curve of her hips, so different from Brandon's bulky frame. Fiona's tongue was in her mouth, her fingers tangled in Nicole's hair. She slid a hand around Fiona's lower back, drawing her closer. Their breasts pressed together, and Nicole's nipples hardened into aching peaks inside her dress.

It had been so long, so very long since she'd been touched by anyone but herself, even longer since she'd felt anything like this. Her skin was alive with sensation, every cell attuned to Fiona's presence, acutely aware of everywhere they touched and the places not yet touching.

"You feel so good," Fiona murmured, one hand sliding down Nicole's back to cup her ass.

"So do you." Nicole drew her closer still, so that their hips brushed together.

Fiona slid one of her thighs between Nicole's, and she groaned at the contact, unable to hold back as she rolled her hips, seeking friction. Fiona tightened the hand on Nicole's ass, encouraging her, and she rolled her hips again, clutching at any part of Fiona she could reach.

"Yes," she gasped. "More."

Fiona took Nicole's hands in hers and drew her down to the marble beneath them. "Anything you want," she whispered.

"What do *you* want?" Nicole countered, a tingle of nerves mixing with the desire overwhelming her system, because Fiona clearly had more experience in these matters than she did, and she hated feeling inadequate.

"You." Fiona captured her mouth in another breathless kiss.

Nicole had thought Fiona's eyes to be sky blue before, but this close, she saw that there was a gold ring around her pupil, mirroring their tropical paradise where the turquoise water met the golden sand. Her eyes were the beach, not the sky.

And her body promised the answers to everything Nicole had been seeking.

"I've never done this before," she whispered into their kiss.

Fiona nodded as though she'd already known this. She peppered a string of gentle kisses over Nicole's cheek to her jaw. "Are you sure it's what you want?"

"Yes, but…" Her fingers clenched in the soft fabric of Fiona's dress.

"But?" Fiona held her in her direct stare.

"A little nervous, I guess."

Fiona rested a hand on Nicole's hip, squeezing gently. "No need to be."

"You'll tell me if I'm doing it wrong?"

Laughter danced in Fiona's eyes. "You couldn't possibly." She took one of Nicole's hands and pressed it against her chest. Her heart raced against Nicole's palm. "Feel that? You drive me mad every time you touch me, every time you so much as look at me."

"Oh," Nicole whispered, her own heart speeding at the contact, desire throbbing in her core.

Fiona leaned in for another kiss. "You'll be fine. But we don't have to do anything you don't want to do."

"Oh, I want to." She was so turned on, she might combust if Fiona didn't touch her soon.

"Me too," Fiona whispered, sliding her hands down Nicole's back so that their bodies pressed together. "It's okay if you're just using me to forget your ex-husband. I don't mind."

Nicole shook her head emphatically. "It's not that. Or maybe that's part of it. But I've known for a long time that I'm bisexual, if that's what you're asking. I had a girlfriend in college."

"But you never had sex with her?"

"No. We were young and unsure of ourselves. It never went that far."

Fiona smiled at her, a wicked grin full of sinful promise. "Then I'll be your first."

6

Fiona trailed a hand down Nicole's body, positively high with anticipation over giving Nicole her first sexual experience with a woman. "This will be our warm-up," she whispered against Nicole's neck, causing gooseflesh to rise on her skin. "Later, we'll make a proper bed out of those thermal suits, and we can take our time."

"Fuck," Nicole whispered, back arching as Fiona's fingers traced the edge of her underwear.

"Mm." Fiona tugged at her panties. "We need to get rid of these."

Nicole pushed them down her legs, drawing Fiona in for another kiss as their bodies pressed together, and she thought she'd never seen anything as lovely and pure as this vision of Nicole, eyes hot and wanting, her hair a mess of dark waves around her face as Greek columns rose behind her and the ocean crashed below on the beach.

Fiona couldn't help picturing what they looked like together up here, lying above the sea in this crumbling pavilion, the contrast of her red dress against the gray of

Nicole's. If it were a painting, she'd hang it in her living room, a masterpiece to inspire her day in and day out.

Smiling at the thought, she slid forward, rolling Nicole onto her back. "Sorry about the marble," she whispered as she positioned herself over Nicole.

"I don't even feel it." Her hips lifted, seeking contact with Fiona's.

"You probably will later, but I'll make it worth your while." She wanted Nicole naked, wanted to touch and kiss every bare inch of her, but that would have to wait, because it simply wasn't practical on this ancient, filthy marble. Instead, she palmed one of Nicole's breasts through her dress while her other hand slid beneath her skirt. Her fingers brushed against Nicole's drenched flesh. "You're so wet for me."

"Yes," she whispered, hips thrusting to increase the pressure of Fiona's touch.

Giving her what she wanted, Fiona began to stroke her. She gathered Nicole's arousal on her fingers and swirled it over her clit, drawing a strangled sound from Nicole. Their faces met for a messy kiss as Fiona built a rhythm with her fingers. She pushed two fingers inside Nicole, stroking in and out as her palm provided friction against her clit.

Nicole writhed against the marble, eyes closed, mouth slightly open, eyebrows jumping as she drew closer to her release. Fiona curled her fingers, pressing against Nicole's G-spot, and she let out a needy whimper that had Fiona pressing her own thighs together. She resisted the urge to straddle Nicole, giving herself some much-needed relief.

This moment was all about Nicole.

Fiona bent her head, kissing Nicole's neck as she focused her full attention on delivering a shattering finish. She wanted Nicole's first experience with a woman to be memorable for all the right reasons. Fiona quickened her pace, dividing her attention between Nicole's G-spot and her clit, and Nicole flung an arm over her eyes, swearing, her thighs clamped around Fiona's hand. Fiona added a third finger, and Nicole's body gripped her, hard.

"Fuck," she gasped, hips moving frantically as her body spasmed around Fiona's fingers. Fiona held herself still, allowing Nicole to ride out the waves of her release until she fell limp against the marble, her pussy still pulsing against Fiona's hand. "Wow."

"I'll say." Fiona carefully withdrew her hand. She leaned in to press another kiss against Nicole's lips, trying to ignore the insistent throbbing in her core and the wetness pooling in her panties. This was Nicole's first time, and she might not be ready to return the favor just yet.

It had been a while since Fiona had been with a woman, long enough that she'd almost forgotten how much she enjoyed it, even when she was the one giving and not receiving. Generally, she always preferred women, but her number one preference was for no-strings-attached sex, and that was usually easier to find with a man. So she'd grown accustomed to burying her desires and making do with what she could get.

Nicole was the living embodiment of every one of Fiona's fantasies, and she wasn't sure she'd ever been so turned on without having been touched. So much that she could almost come just from shifting her thighs together and watching Nicole regain her wits after her orgasm.

"That was...amazing." Nicole rolled toward her. "My turn?"

"Please," Fiona whispered, almost overwhelmed in anticipation of Nicole's touch. She lay beside her, body burning as Nicole raked her gaze from the wild tangle of her hair to her chipped red-painted toes.

"So beautiful," Nicole said as she slid a hand experimentally over Fiona's chest.

Fiona was too turned on to do anything but arch her back, pressing her tit into Nicole's palm. She whimpered as Nicole squeezed her nipple through the bodice of her dress.

"Glad you cut this," Nicole said, bringing her other hand to the jagged hemline of the altered red dress.

"Me too," she gasped, hips jerking toward Nicole's hand.

Nicole tugged at her underwear. "Can I take these off?"

Fiona lifted her hips as Nicole slid them down her legs, feeling a rush of cool air against her overheated flesh. Nicole leaned over her, eyes narrowed in concentration as she brushed a hand against her, fingers dipping into the wetness she found there. Fiona closed her eyes as a sigh of relief escaped her lips.

"Wow," Nicole murmured, dipping her head to trail her lips over Fiona's chest. "You feel different... Better than I expected."

Fiona rolled her hips against Nicole's hand, silently urging her to continue, and Nicole seemed to take the hint. She pressed her fingers against Fiona's clit, sending her brain whirling. *Yes.* God, she'd needed so badly to be touched. She'd needed to feel a woman's touch, and ever since she'd first laid eyes on Nicole in the *Cyprus Star*'s bar three nights ago, she'd needed to feel *this* woman's touch.

Nicole settled into a rhythm, imitating the way Fiona had touched her, which was really fucking good, but frankly, it wouldn't have mattered what Nicole did at this point. Fiona was so close, she could come from pretty much anything Nicole chose to do to her.

"Tell me if there's something you like," Nicole murmured, spreading kisses over her neck.

"You're doing just fine," Fiona managed, hips moving, breath tangled in her throat as her body spiraled toward release. Her orgasm coiled inside her, hot and tight, making her tremble in anticipation. As much as she wanted to tumble headfirst into release, she didn't want this to end so soon, and the tiny part of her brain left to rational thought knew that if she came now, it would be over almost embarrassingly fast.

As if sensing her thoughts, Nicole slowed her rhythm, her fingers ghosting over Fiona's clit as she focused instead on kissing her, her free hand exploring Fiona's body while she grumbled in frustration.

"Patience," Nicole whispered.

"Not my strong suit," she mumbled, breathless.

Nicole laughed against her neck. "I like seeing you like this. So sexy."

"Killing me."

Nicole sucked at the pulse point on her neck, swiping one finger over her clit, and Fiona was spinning again. Nicole returned to her previous rhythm with a vengeance, her fingers everywhere Fiona needed them. Pressure built inside her, so hot and tight she could hardly stand it. Her hips bucked, her eyes slammed shut, and then she was coming.

Release ignited in her core, radiating through her body, pulsing through her in blissful waves that left her limp and breathless, trembling in pleasure.

"That was, without a doubt, the most beautiful thing I've ever seen," Nicole said, sounding awed.

Fiona cracked open an eye to look up at her. "You're really fucking good at this."

Nicole smiled widely. "Not bad for my first time?"

"Not bad?" Fiona blew out a breath, her body still trembling with the aftershocks of her orgasm. "I haven't come that hard in...too long to remember."

Nicole lay beside her, one arm sliding around Fiona's waist to draw her close. "This was amazing."

They lay there like that for a while, neither of them moving or speaking, just breathing in the closeness and comfort between them. Well, Nicole's body was comforting, but the cold marble beneath Fiona's ass and digging into her skull left something to be desired.

"As much as I'd like to stay here and discover all the different ways to make you come, we're meant to be doing something," she murmured, stroking her hand down Nicole's back.

"We are?"

She nodded. "The sun's already halfway to noon, and we need to find out if we're on an island or not."

"You're right." Nicole drew herself together with impressive speed, sitting up and grabbing her underwear. "Round two tonight?"

"Count on it." Fiona grabbed her own panties and followed Nicole to the beach, where they cleaned up before continuing on their journey. Hand in hand, they walked the beach, not a leisurely stroll but walking with purpose, fueled by the desire to be saved, to go home, to share a real bed together at some point in the near future.

Several times, they had to detour around rocky outcrops and other obstructions to the shoreline, but overall the coast was clear, so to speak. They looped consistently to the right as they walked, so much so that Fiona wasn't the least bit surprised when the rock they'd slept on last night came into view.

"Island," she said matter-of-factly.

Nicole sighed. "Damn."

"It's okay." Fiona gave her hand a squeeze. "Someone's going to find us."

"But in the meantime," Nicole said, her face set in determination. "We need to get a few things done."

"What do you have in mind?"

"We need to start a fire, try our hand at fishing, search again for a source of fresh water, and move our base camp down to the ruins."

Fiona frowned at the enormity of the tasks Nicole had set forth. "Yes. Okay."

"I think fire and fishing should come first," Nicole said. "We've still got plenty of water in our emergency rations, plus a collector tarp in case it rains, and we can sleep here again tonight if we need to."

"I agree. How do you plan to start a fire? Of all the supplies in that boat, there aren't matches."

"Guess they don't intend for people to start fires at sea?" Nicole said with a smile. "But they gave us a signal mirror, and I'm going to use that to try to get one started."

"I'd say your fire-starting skills are top-notch," Fiona said with a meaningful look. "I suppose I'll have a go at fishing, then."

NICOLE STARED, awestruck, at the tiny flame curling around the dried grass she'd placed in her makeshift fire pit, feeling like a superhero. She hadn't expected it to be this easy, but the grass had begun to smoke almost as soon as she'd aimed the mirror's reflection at it. Except, as it turned out, her celebration was short-lived, because the flame evaporated in a puff of smoke a few seconds later. But if she'd done it once, she could do it again, and next time, she'd be better prepared with things to feed it.

In her mind's eye, she saw the pile of red fabric Fiona had left inside the lifeboat. A scrap or two from the dress might keep the flame going long enough for it to catch some of her bigger kindling on fire.

Fiona's red dress. Nicole couldn't stop thinking about their encounter in the pavilion, replaying every moment in her head, reliving the pleasure they'd given each other. How had they managed to create something so beautiful out of such an impossible situation? A tingle of anticipation raced through her as she thought of the night to come.

Fighting back a dreamy smile, she walked toward the lifeboat, stopping dead in her tracks as she spotted Fiona in the surf with the fishing tackle, wearing...not much. She'd tied a strip of red fabric around her breasts and another, larger piece around her hips as a makeshift skirt. And she looked...hot. Like, ridiculously hot.

"I like the new outfit," she called.

Fiona turned, and Nicole lost her breath. The red fabric covered only the most essential parts of her, knotted at her right hip in a way that made it clear she wasn't wearing anything underneath. A red jewel winked from her belly button.

"Holy shit," Nicole spluttered. "I really am shipwrecked with a goddess."

"I couldn't spend another moment in that dress," Fiona said with a shrug. "This is much more comfortable."

"Very nice to look at too."

"Help yourself if you want to do the same," Fiona said, returning her attention to the fishing line in her hand.

"I just might." Because Nicole could barely stand her dress after almost four days in it. "Catch anything yet?"

Fiona shook her head. "Had a few nibbles, though. My bait keeps falling off."

"What are you using?"

"I found some kind of mollusk attached to those rocks over there and smashed it open."

"Gross." Nicole scrunched her face. "But good thinking."

She leaned into the lifeboat and grabbed a couple of thin strips of fabric, which she carried up the beach to her fire pit. Luckily, the fabric had caught some sun earlier and dried out. She'd built their fire in the middle of the "O" in their SOS, hollowing out a spot in the sand and filling it with small dry sticks and grass. Determined, she lifted the mirror, aiming it at a fresh section of her kindling. Again, it began to smoke, and after a minute, a tiny flame burst to life.

Crouching down, she sprinkled more dry grass on it, nursing the flame bigger. Once it had grown about two inches tall, she dangled a strip of fabric so that it just touched the tip of the flame. For a moment, her baby fire flickered as if it might go out, but then the fabric began to burn, and whoa, Fiona's dress was alarmingly flammable. Flames licked up the strip Nicole held, and she dropped it into the fire pit, letting it simmer with the rest of the kindling.

She added the second strip, and then some small sticks, and before long, she had an honest-to-God fire going. She sat patiently, adding increasingly larger sticks until finally, even the tree limb she'd carried over was burning.

"Impressive," Fiona said from behind her, and Nicole turned to see her holding two small fish. She held them up. "It's not much, but they'll taste better than that god-awful stuff in the food rations, although it turns out the fish quite like it."

"You baited them with our food ration?" Nicole couldn't fight her smile.

She nodded. "They can have it all, if they keep getting on my line."

"We're really rocking this castaway thing, aren't we?"

Fiona lifted an eyebrow. "Indeed."

Nicole's gaze shifted behind her and sharpened. "Holy shit."

"What?" Fiona looked over her shoulder. "Oh my God."

A boat was visible on the horizon.

7

F iona lifted the flare above her head and fired. With a sizzling sound, it soared into the sky above, leaving an arc of red sparks in its wake.

"Please please please..." Nicole chanted, hands clasped in front of her chest.

The boat was far enough away that Fiona couldn't see it clearly, but it seemed to have the shape of a small fishing vessel. Was it close enough for the fishermen to see the flare?

"Get the mirror," she said, and Nicole dashed up the beach to grab it.

She stood beside Fiona, aiming it this way and that, attempting to create a flash of light that might catch the fishermen's attention. Overhead, the flare fizzled into a trail of gray smoke that drifted with the sea breeze.

"I can't tell if they've seen us," Nicole said.

Neither could Fiona. She stood there quietly, hands at her sides as Nicole moved the mirror, but the boat didn't appear to change course. Nicole kept going, waving tirelessly as the boat wavered and disappeared over the curve of the horizon.

"Maybe they've gone for help," she whispered.

Fiona shook her head. "They'd have come this way if they saw us."

"Dammit." Tears shimmered in Nicole's eyes. Her shoulders slumped, and she sat down in the sand.

"Go make yourself a new outfit with the spare fabric," Fiona said quietly. "Take a bath in the ocean and change your clothes. You'll feel much better. Trust me."

With a quick nod, Nicole stood and headed in the direction of the lifeboat.

Fiona clenched her jaw against her own disappointment. They'd wasted one of their two flares. Next time, they'd have to be certain before they fired. Maybe they ought to wait for a boat that passed by during the night. Certainly, the flare would be more visible then, but would fishing boats pass by this area during the night?

She knelt at the fire pit Nicole had made in the middle of their SOS, relieved to see the fire burning steadily despite them abandoning it to chase untouchable ships on the horizon. The fish she'd caught lay on a rock beside it. She rose and carried them to the shore, where she'd left her supplies. Steeling herself, she took the knife and sliced open the fish to remove the nasty bits, making herself gag in the process.

With that accomplished, she strung them on a stick and extended it across the fire. After piling a few nearby rocks beside the fire pit, she was able to leave the fish roasting just above the hungry flames.

"Nice work." Nicole knelt beside her, one arm coming to rest around Fiona's shoulders.

She smiled at the sight of Nicole wearing strips of her dress. "You too."

"It doesn't look nearly as good on me as it does on you," Nicole said with a rueful smile, a hint of sadness still lingering around her eyes.

"I disagree." She let her gaze linger on the swell of Nicole's breasts, barely contained beneath the red fabric she'd tied there, before admiring the swath of fabric around her hips and all the skin and curves left exposed by her new attire. Fiona wanted to lick her from head to foot, with particular attention to the places in between.

"My boobs are going to fall right out of this thing." Nicole tugged at it self-consciously.

Fiona grinned. "I don't mind if they do."

It was true that Nicole had a lot more to contain in that area than Fiona did. Nicole's curves were as endless as they were beautiful, while Fiona was built like an athlete—lean and petite. They sat together as the sun settled low in the sky.

"We'll stay here tonight," Nicole said drowsily, staring into the flames.

"Yes. I'm going to build us a better bed up on that rock before the sun sets." Fiona stood and walked to the lifeboat. She took six of the thermal suits and carried them up the beach to the rock where they'd slept last night. There, she unzipped them all and spread them out like a makeshift blanket.

Good enough.

Carefully, she took the two she and Nicole had slept in last night and zipped them together to make a bigger sack for them to share. Satisfied, she headed back to the beach.

"Let me have a look at your leg before it gets any darker," Nicole said.

Rather than protest, Fiona stopped in front of her to let Nicole inspect it. Fussing about Nicole's fussing only made it worse. It was better to just let her look at the wound and move on.

"Does it hurt?" Nicole asked.

Fiona kept her eyes on the horizon. "Not much."

It did hurt, a lot if she let herself think about it, but she'd had plenty of practice separating her thoughts from the more painful aspects of life. Physical pain wasn't so different from emotional pain that way. The more she ignored it, the easier it became, like strengthening a muscle, and she'd been strengthening this particular muscle most of her life.

"It still looks really red and swollen," Nicole said. "Let me clean it again with one of those disinfectant wipes."

"After supper," Fiona said.

Nicole acquiesced with a smile. "I'm looking forward to supper."

"Me too." Her mouth watered as she looked at the fish, crispy now that they'd hung over the flames for a while. "I'm so hungry right now, I could eat the whole thing, bones and all."

"Same." Nicole lifted the fish clear of the fire. She waved them around for a minute to cool them off before tugging them off the stick one at a time. She handed one to Fiona. "Cheers."

It was a messy business eating whole fish with nothing but their fingers, but neither of them much cared about manners at this point. They poked and picked their way through their meal, licking their fingers shamelessly. Fiona had never been a big fan of seafood, but after three days of lifeboat food rations, it was her favorite thing.

"God, this is so good," Nicole said with a groan of appreciation as she crunched on a crispy fish fin.

"It is," Fiona agreed, sucking the last bit of meat off her finger. The fish had been small, barely larger than the palm of her hand, but either her stomach had shrunk from lack of food or she was in worse health than she realized, because she felt comfortably full after eating it.

"We'll catch more tomorrow," Nicole said cheerfully, a full belly seeming to have displaced the last of her disappointment about the ship they'd seen earlier. "Lots of fish. We'll find water and boil it over our fire, and we'll relocate our camp. We'll be living like goddesses in those ancient ruins until the next fishing boat passes by and spots us."

"That's the spirit," Fiona said with a half-hearted smile. As much as she enjoyed Nicole's company, she really needed some time to herself right now. If they'd been safely on the *Cyprus Star*, she'd have retreated to her cabin or found a quiet nook somewhere. She'd run out of conversation, was too tired for pep talks, and really wanted a hot bath.

Now that Nicole had brought attention to it, the wound on her leg throbbed in time with her pulse, steady and obnoxiously persistent. Combined with her other scrapes and bruises, she could hardly breathe past the scream building in her throat. She was suffocating in her own misery, and she needed to get herself together before she took it out on Nicole.

"Let's pick up this mess, and then I want to clean your leg," Nicole said, as if she'd read Fiona's mind.

"Fine," she said irritably.

Nicole reached over and squeezed her hand in quiet apology. They stood and gathered the remains of their fish, which they buried beneath a pile of small rocks to use as bait tomorrow. There didn't seem to be any animals on the island, but no sense leaving it out to attract scavengers, just in case. They rinsed off in the water before making their way to the lifeboat. Nicole got the flashlight and an antiseptic wipe and gestured for Fiona to sit.

She did, turning her head as Nicole knelt to examine the wound. While she felt foolish about the rest of her bruises from her needless fall when they launched the boat, this one had been acquired while she scaled the railing after releasing the safety pins, so at least there was no guilt to harbor about it.

"It's definitely infected," Nicole said, worry in her tone. "I don't know what else to do but keep trying to clean it. Salt is good for wounds, right? So maybe wash it in the ocean more often tomorrow."

"Okay." Fiona glanced down, seeing the wound clearly in the beam of the flashlight. It was red and swollen, just as Nicole had said, and the area between the adhesive strips looked yellowish with pus. Fiona's stomach curdled, and she cursed herself silently for looking. She'd never had a very strong stomach for these things, particularly on her own body. She gritted her teeth when Nicole rubbed at it with the antiseptic wipe, fingers clenched around the edge of the seat to keep herself from screaming in pain and frustration.

"All done," Nicole announced, patting her thigh as she stood.

Fiona turned and snagged a packet of aspirin out of the first aid kit before Nicole closed it, again grateful when she said nothing while Fiona swallowed the pills.

"We're lucky to have water rations for eighteen people," Nicole said instead, handing her a new water pack.

"Yes."

They climbed out of the lifeboat together just as the sun dipped below the horizon, leaving them in its purplish shadow.

"I'm going to put more wood on the fire," Nicole said.

"Do you think it will keep overnight?"

She shrugged. "I might come down and tend to it one more time before I fall asleep."

"I'll help too if I wake up during the night."

"Worst case, I'll start a new one tomorrow," Nicole said. "It wasn't as hard as I thought it would be."

"You're turning into a regular survivalist," Fiona said with a smile, her mood softening. She stopped next to the rock where she'd done her morning meditation and yoga. "You go ahead. I'll catch up."

Nicole paused, hesitation in her eyes, but then she nodded and walked ahead alone.

NICOLE SAT on the blanket of survival suits Fiona had made for them, watching her as she sat alone on the beach. There was a switch inside her that flipped throughout the day, transforming her from the woman who'd clung to Nicole as she came around her fingers to this other person who withdrew inside herself and fiercely needed to be alone.

And it was okay. Nicole was happy to give her space or comfort or anything at all she could give. It was just that right now, as the sun faded away on their second night on the island, their fourth night since kidnappers boarded the *Cyprus Star* and turned their lives upside down, Nicole felt incredibly alone and terrified and overwhelmed.

She wrapped her arms around herself and squeezed her eyes shut against the urge to cry. Fiona's leg worried her. If the infection spread, what would happen? She couldn't lose her. Not now. Maybe not ever.

"Pretty, isn't it?"

She turned, not having heard Fiona come up behind

her. Nicole followed her gaze to the moon hanging silvery bright over the ocean below. "Yeah."

Fiona sat beside her, her fingers finding Nicole's in the semidarkness.

"Better?" Nicole asked, knowing her question needed no explanation.

"Yes," Fiona said softly. "Thanks."

"Do you think they're looking for us?"

"No," Fiona answered. "I doubt anyone knows what's become of us."

"Dammit." Nicole blew out a breath in frustration.

"But they're going to find us anyway," Fiona said. "Fishermen were out there today, and more will come tomorrow."

"Our families must be worried sick." Nicole finally voiced the worry that had been eating at her. It was easy for her and Fiona to get caught up in the nightmare of their reality, but what were their families going through? "Do they think we're being held hostage on the boat? Do they know we're missing?"

Fiona was silent, her eyes cast downward at her lap.

"Who's missing you tonight, Fi?" she asked quietly.

"No one, most likely," came her answer, spoken so softly, Nicole could barely make out the words.

"That's not possible. Someone's missing you," she said fiercely, wrapping an arm around Fiona's shoulders. "I'd be missing you like crazy. Don't you have any family?"

"My father, but we're not close." Some volume had returned to her voice, but she still didn't sound quite like herself.

"Is it because..." She gestured between them.

"Because I'm queer?" Fiona laughed bitterly. "No, although I don't think he's crazy about that either."

"Well, if your dad knows you're missing at sea, I'm sure

he's worried sick, no matter what's happened between you in the past."

Fiona stared at the rapidly darkening sky, her expression unreadable.

"I'm sorry," Nicole whispered over the lump that had grown in her throat.

"For what?" Fiona turned to look at her, eyes glistening with the reflection of the moon.

"For whatever happened with your family, for you thinking no one in the world would miss you, for being stood up by that man this week." Any and all of it. She felt fiercely attached to this woman she'd known only a few days, a woman who seemed to take no attachments of her own and would probably walk away without a backward glance when and if they were rescued.

"Don't," Fiona whispered, turning to press her lips against Nicole's.

"I can't help it."

Fiona deepened the kiss, her tongue sliding into Nicole's mouth. If she was trying to distract Nicole, it was working. She tasted like sea salt and the breath mints from Nicole's purse, and she felt like heaven as her arms wrapped around Nicole. They'd be quite a sight if anyone passed by their island right now, limbs tangled in the moonlight as they lay atop their silvery web of thermal suits, wearing matching scraps of red fabric like modern-day loincloths.

"There's something I've been thinking about since we left those ruins this morning," Nicole whispered into her mouth.

"Mm?" Fiona raised her left knee—the good knee—so that it pressed into the heat between Nicole's legs, scrambling her thoughts.

"I want to taste you."

Fiona's chest expanded as she sucked in a breath. "Oh." She breathed deeply, her eyes locked on Nicole's. "Yes. Please."

"So polite." Nicole grinned, dropping her head to kiss her again.

"I'm a proper English girl, what can I say?"

Nicole *had* been thinking about it since this morning, but now, having just witnessed such an unexpected and emotional glimpse into Fiona's past, she wanted more than ever to give her pleasure, to do what she could to take away her pain, to make sure she knew that at least one other person in this universe cared about her.

Nicole cared about her an awful damn lot.

"Lose this," she said, tugging at the red fabric on Fiona's body. As Fiona rose up on her elbows to unknot the fabric, Nicole untied her own, casting it aside. She sat on her knees, staring down at Fiona's naked body, thinking she'd never seen anything so gorgeous. The jewel in her belly ring winked in the moonlight. "I need to see this more tomorrow in the daylight," she said, twirling it beneath her fingers.

"Gladly," Fiona murmured, her hips shifting restlessly.

Nicole dropped her head and kissed the jewel while one of her hands slipped between Fiona's thighs, finding her already wet. A sigh escaped her lips, as if this simple touch brought her unspeakable pleasure. Why did she live such a solitary life when she had so much love and passion to give?

Nicole started at her breasts, exploring with her tongue, thrilled by the way Fiona pressed against her, nipples hardening beneath her lips. Nicole placed wet kisses down her stomach as her fingers stroked Fiona, eventually settling between her thighs. She'd thought about this moment occasionally over the years, what it would be like to give—and receive—oral sex with a woman. And now she found herself filled with a fluttery sense of anticipation.

She gave an experimental lick, and Fiona's flavor exploded on her tongue, sharp and salty like the ocean she'd so recently bathed in. Nicole drew her tongue between her folds, and any insecurities she might have harbored about her ability to do this melted away as Fiona moaned, one hand clutched loosely in Nicole's hair, back arched in breathless pleasure.

Nicole settled into an easy rhythm, licking and sucking, completely entranced by the way Fiona writhed and gasped, the muscles in her thighs beginning to shake as she grew nearer to her release. Nicole shifted her position and pushed first one, then a second finger inside Fiona's body, transferring the full attention of her mouth to her clit. She created suction with her lips as her tongue swirled, and Fiona rose up onto her elbows.

"Fuck me," she gasped, staring down at Nicole with eyes as dewy as the night around them.

Nicole smiled with her eyes as she took Fiona right over the edge. She cried out as her body clamped around Nicole's fingers, pulsing again and again as she came.

"Jesus Christ." Fiona collapsed on the blanket beneath her. "You're a goddamn rock star."

"And you're a flatterer." Nicole kissed her way up Fiona's body to her mouth, letting her taste herself on Nicole's tongue.

"On the contrary," Fiona murmured, kissing her back. "I'm not prone to flattery."

"Could have fooled me."

"I just really fucking like you," Fiona whispered, and the words did funny things in Nicole's chest, making her feel warm and full, as if she might explode from the power of them.

"I really fucking like you too." She snaked an arm around Fiona's waist, giving her a squeeze. They held on to each other for a long minute as Fiona caught her breath.

Then she propped herself up on one elbow, grinning wickedly as she rolled Nicole beneath her so their naked bodies pressed together in a tangle of wetness and heat and desire.

"Your leg," Nicole gasped.

"Fuck it," Fiona responded.

"No. I need you in top form tomorrow, Fi. We've got an island to escape."

"Fine," Fiona said, rolling to her back. "On your knees, then."

"What?" She gasped as her brain caught up to what Fiona was suggesting. "Oh, I don't know…"

"It's the easiest way," Fiona said coyly. "If you're so concerned about my leg."

"Oh my God," Nicole whispered as she got onto her hands and knees, crawling up Fiona's body. "This is insane."

"Not at all," Fiona murmured, trailing kisses down Nicole's stomach as she got into position, and okay, she felt more than a little self-conscious about crouching over Fiona's face, even in the dark and even knowing it was for the benefit of her wounded leg.

And then Fiona's tongue skimmed over her sensitive flesh, and she forgot all that, because *holy shit*. She settled her hips a bit lower, and Fiona gripped her thighs, holding her where she wanted her as her tongue began to work some kind of magic that had Nicole seeing stars almost immediately.

She moaned, dropped her head, and moaned again. The

rock beneath their thermal suits bit into her knees, but she barely felt it as Fiona's tongue swirled, plunging into her body before retreating to circle her clit, and *oh God...*

"I'm so close," she gasped, sitting her hips back a little farther, all modesty forgotten as her insides twined and her heart raced and sweat slicked her body. In response, Fiona picked up the pace, putting her full effort into giving Nicole as much pleasure as possible, or at least that was how it felt.

She could hear herself panting and gasping, her hips rolling against Fiona's tongue, her body lit as brightly as the moon hanging silvery white over the ocean to her left. She moaned as the orgasm burst through her in hot, pulsing waves that left her shaking in its aftermath. She rolled onto the blanket beside Fiona, eyes closed, gasping as pleasure flowed through her as powerfully as the ocean's tides.

It's so good. Nicole breathed past tears, her chest swelling with all kinds of warm, mushy things, feelings that ran so much deeper and stronger than she ought to be feeling for Fiona, given the circumstances.

8

F iona stood naked in the moonlight, watching as Nicole poked another stick into the fire. "Be careful," she couldn't help saying, envisioning sparks pricking at Nicole's exposed flesh.

"I am," she said over her shoulder with a smile.

They'd spent the past hours delivering several memorable orgasms to each other, and now, exhausted yet rejuvenated, they'd come down to the beach to attend to final matters before bed. Fiona waded into the ocean to relieve herself and wash the sweat and sex from her body.

Nicole joined her, yelping as the water touched her skin. "Aren't you afraid something's going to bite you?"

"You mean, other than me?"

"Like a shark," Nicole said earnestly. "Or even just a crab."

"No," Fiona said. "I'll take my chances."

Nicole crouched down and gave herself a quick rinse. "Okay, I'm clean, and now I'm getting the fuck out of here before something eats me."

Laughing, Fiona followed her onto the beach. They used

the remnants of her dress to dry off, and then climbed together to the top of their rock. Fiona held up the two thermal suits she'd zipped together earlier. Now that night had fallen, the ocean breeze had gone from cool to cold, and they were both shivering after their dip in the ocean.

"Perfect," Nicole whispered as she crawled inside.

Fiona slipped in behind her, resting one hand comfortably on Nicole's stomach. "Look up."

"What?" Nicole rolled to her back and gasped. "Oh."

Above them, the sky gleamed with an impossible number of stars, as if they could see all the way to the ends of the universe. "Beautiful, isn't it?"

"It's magical," Nicole agreed. "In the city, it's so bright, I'm lucky if I can see the moon some nights."

"I've always loved stargazing," Fiona said. "I can see a lot from my house, but not like this."

"Is that the Milky Way?" Nicole's voice was awestruck.

"I think so." Fiona stared at the twinkling band of stars overhead, so thick, she couldn't tell one from the next.

"What's that?" Nicole asked. "It looks like one of the stars is...moving."

Fiona looked where she was pointing. "It's a satellite."

"You can see them?" Nicole asked, incredulous.

"Mm-hmm. You can see the space station too when it passes overhead. It's quite something."

"That's crazy. And really cool."

"It is."

They lay there together in silence, gazing up at the stars. "I thought you were blind without your contacts," Nicole said finally.

"I'm farsighted. I can see the stars, but I can't read a book."

"Oh," Nicole whispered. "I'm not used to being

unplugged. I feel kind of embarrassed to admit I never took the time to do stuff like this before."

"It's time worth taking," Fiona murmured. No screen or gadget could beat the feeling of lying here beneath this blanket of stars with Nicole in her arms.

"Remind me of this once we're home, will you? In case I forget."

"You won't forget."

"That day on the *Cyprus Star*? I spent most of it checking emails from work. That's why my phone was almost dead by the time we got into the lifeboat."

"All work and no play," Fiona chastised gently.

"It's true. I was just so...driven. I mean, I love my job, but now that I'm away from it, I see how it had overtaken my life."

"Mm."

"I was so busy marketing investment portfolios, I didn't notice my husband was fucking another woman."

"I'm sorry," Fiona murmured.

"It's okay," Nicole said. "It really is. We hadn't been happy together for a long time. We're better off apart."

Fiona gave her a squeeze, unsure what to say. She'd never been in a relationship long enough to become unhappy, but she couldn't imagine ever feeling that way about Nicole.

"I could lie here like this with you all night," Nicole whispered.

"Same." If she weren't so exhausted, she might have too. As it was, she drifted into a deep, dreamless sleep. She woke with the sun, coming to her senses bit by bit, first aware of the steady rhythm of Nicole's breathing, the scent of her hair, the warmth of her body. Fiona felt warm, inside and out, full in a way she hadn't felt in longer than she could remember.

Nicole had done this to her, slipped past her defenses and crawled inside her psyche, offering pleasure and comfort in equal measure. It was all more and less than Fiona wanted. She'd always yearned for something—or perhaps someone—to ground her, and for today, she was content to let that person be Nicole.

When they got home—and Fiona truly believed they would get home—Nicole would go back to New York, hopefully not back to her husband, because he sounded like a dick, but she was still reeling from the divorce. She needed to get her feet under her, work out who she was and what she wanted.

It wouldn't be Fiona. She was just a distraction, a piece in the puzzle of Nicole's post-divorce adventure to find herself. A rebound, wasn't that what they called it? Nicole was exploring her sexuality, and then fate threw them into this crazy situation that had turned both of their worlds upside down.

Eventually, they'd be right side up again. Fiona would return to her cottage in Nice. She'd paint for herself and create digital graphics to pay the bills. She needed the quiet structure of the life she'd created. Solitude was her solace. Her home was her oasis. France was her home beacon.

Once she made it back, she absolutely would not think of Nicole or New York or the way it felt to lie here inside this sleeping bag, curled around her perfect, sleeping form. Fiona drew in a deep breath and pushed it out, cleansing herself of her melancholy.

It was just that she hadn't spent this much time with someone in a long time. Fiona didn't like most people very much. She needed space. She needed the structure of her routines. Yesterday, she'd slipped away without a second thought, meditated on the beach as the sun rose, calming the chaos in her brain.

This morning, she couldn't bring herself to let go of Nicole and climb out of this safe, warm cocoon they'd created together. So she let her eyes slide shut as she held on to Nicole for just a little while longer.

"Wake up, sleepyhead," Nicole whispered.

Fiona's eyes fluttered open. The sun was fully up now. Nicole had spun to face her inside the sleeping bag and was staring at her with unabashed affection, her hazel eyes gleaming as warm as the earth around them.

"Drifted off waiting for you to wake up," she mumbled sleepily, drawing Nicole closer.

"Sure, you did," Nicole said with a smile, leaning in for a kiss. "I need to go check on the fire."

"Details," Fiona murmured.

"Important details. I don't want to have to start from scratch." She unzipped the suit, letting cool morning air wash over them.

Fiona appreciated the view of Nicole's body as she climbed out of their bed. Maybe she'd ask Nicole to sit nearby while she meditated this morning so she could use her as a focal point. And maybe she was being a lovesick idiot. She sat up, gathering her wits.

Nicole gasped. "Oh God. Your leg."

"It feels better," Fiona responded absentmindedly before she heard the alarm in Nicole's voice. She looked down and saw the yellowish liquid that streaked her lower leg, running from the wound. Her stomach lurched, and she gagged, looking away.

"Shit." Nicole crouched beside her.

"It really does feel better," Fiona said breathlessly, refusing to look again.

"Don't try to placate me," Nicole said firmly. "This is serious, Fi."

"I'm being serious," she insisted. "Last night, I was placating you. This morning, it doesn't hurt nearly as much."

"But..."

"It looks disgusting," Fiona finished for her. "I don't know if that's good or bad. I don't." Except now that she was sitting up, she was afraid she did know, and it wasn't good. Her body felt weak and lethargic, and she ached in places that weren't bruised or cut. Maybe there was nothing sentimental about her sleeping in with Nicole this morning instead of heading to the beach at sunrise. Maybe the infection had worsened.

Nicole reached over and pressed a hand against her forehead. "You don't feel warm."

"I will if you keep touching me." She batted her lashes, attempting to deflect Nicole's concern.

"Don't do that." Nicole's eyes were serious, refusing to be distracted. "I'm worried."

"I know you are." She looked away, focusing on the sun as it crawled up the sky. "So am I. But there's nothing we can do about it."

"I wish I knew what to do. Maybe we ought to take off the bandages and let it drain?"

"Maybe." Fiona forced herself to take another quick glance, her stomach going sour. "God, I'm such a squeamish baby about these things. You do it."

Nicole reached down without hesitation and tugged the three bandages off in quick succession. Each tug met a sharp pain that radiated through her leg. Fiona lay back on their bed, head swimming. "Okay, now it hurts."

"Shit." Nicole bent down, looking at the wound more closely. "What if that was the wrong thing to do?"

"Second-guessing yourself won't do either of us any good."

"No, it won't." Nicole sat back up. "It doesn't smell bad, and I think that must be a good sign."

"You smelled it?" Fiona asked, horrified.

"Well, I mean...my face was pretty close, and I didn't smell anything." She slapped Fiona's shoulder. "I'm just trying to help."

"I know. Thank you." Fiona flung an arm over her eyes, still feeling lightheaded. Her whole leg pulsed with pain.

"It's draining more now, so we'll keep an eye on it this morning and see what happens. Maybe you should take it easy today."

"That's not really an option, is it?" Fiona collected herself and sat up, carefully keeping her eyes on Nicole.

"Sure it is. I'll fish while you tend the fire. Everything else can wait. Maybe we'll get rescued today anyway."

"I'm not going to sit around while you do all the work—"

"I need you healthy," Nicole interrupted. "I couldn't take it if anything happened to you, Fi, and you've more than pulled your weight out here, despite being injured. Just let me take the lead today, okay?"

Fiona sagged against the rock, all the fight draining out of her. "Fine."

NICOLE GRUMBLED under her breath as she wielded the fishing line. Behind her, Fiona sat on her meditation rock, quietly enduring the break Nicole had insisted she take, silver space cape fluttering about her shoulders. She'd sat motionless for what had to be close to an hour now, as Nicole tossed the fishing line over and over with no results.

She was tired and irritable, hungry to the point that she felt like her stomach was going to start digesting itself and sick to death of eating food rations from the lifeboat. Yes, she was grateful they had them, but ugh, they were disgusting.

"I suck at fishing," she announced finally, stomping her foot in the knee-high water and splashing her makeshift skirt in the process.

"But you look very lovely while you're trying," Fiona responded.

"I thought you were meditating."

"I was, using you as my focal point."

"Hmph." Nicole tossed the line again, watching as the hook drifted toward the sandy bottom.

"Sure you don't want me to give it another go?" Fiona asked.

Nicole reined in her foul mood. She wasn't doing either of them any favors if she let her temper get the best of her. It was only going to make it harder to keep Fiona from helping out, and probably harder to catch fish too. "I may not be a doctor, but even I know you're supposed to keep wounds dry while they heal. I shouldn't have let you fish yesterday either."

"You also told me salt's good for wounds, right?" Fiona took her left foot—the good one—and dragged it through the sand, tracing a design with her toes.

"For a rinse," Nicole said. "Not while you stand around fishing, and not while it's draining like that."

Fiona looked away. If the situation hadn't been worrying

her to death, Nicole might have been amused by how grossed out Fiona was about her own wound.

"I was fishing much closer to sunset," she said finally. "Maybe that's the difference."

"Maybe. I haven't had so much as a nibble."

"Then we're wasting time," Fiona said. "Let's get something else accomplished and come back to fishing later. We can have a food ration for breakfast instead."

"Fine." With a sigh, Nicole reeled in the line and coiled it loosely in her hands. She set it inside the lifeboat and pulled out two food rations, which she carried with her to the rock where Fiona sat. Several uncomfortable thoughts were swirling in her mind, but she wasn't sure how to broach them.

"Spit it out," Fiona said with a piqued look.

Nicole ripped open her breakfast. "What?"

"Whatever's got you looking so bothered." Fiona unwrapped her food cube and took a bite.

"It's just, while I was out there fishing, I was thinking about how we're in this little inlet here that's kind of enclosed. Maybe it's hard for passing boats to see us. Maybe it's hard for us to see them. We don't have a very wide view of the sea out there."

"You're absolutely right," Fiona said with a nod. "After breakfast, we should move camp down the beach to the ruins like we'd discussed yesterday."

"But your leg..."

"I can walk just as well as you can," she said firmly. "If it increases our chances of being rescued, I don't think we have a choice, do you?"

"I guess not." Nicole chewed through the rest of her food ration in silence. They'd eaten about a quarter of their supply now and drunk over half their water. Should they start rationing more strictly? At what point did they decide to take their chances and head out in the lifeboat again, hoping to rescue themselves rather than wait for it to come to them? With Fiona's leg steadily worsening, they might not have much time to decide.

"What should we do about the fire?" Fiona asked when they'd finished eating.

"That spot is about an hour's walk from here. I don't think I could keep a burning stick going that long. We might have to start a new one there."

"I think it's less than an hour," Fiona said pensively. "But you're right, it's probably not practical to bring this one with us."

"Maybe we should build it up before we go, though, just in case I can't get a new fire started."

They spent the next few minutes planning what to take and what to leave, what was worth coming back for on a second trip and what they could do without. As had become their post-meal custom, they rinsed their mouths in the surf and followed it with a breath mint from Nicole's purse. The mints would run out in a few days, but they'd have more important problems if they were still out here in a few days than fresh breath for kissing.

Speaking of kissing...

Fiona's hand tugged at the red fabric knotted at Nicole's hip, and she turned, her hands automatically gravitating to Fiona's body, settling into the now-familiar dip of her waist. Their noses bumped as they leaned in, mouths seeking, hungry for the comfort they'd find in the heat of a kiss, freedom from worries and fears, uncertainty over what lay ahead.

They kissed as if their lives depended on it, and maybe theirs did, because with Fiona's tongue in her mouth,

Fiona's fingers crawling beneath the red sash tied around her hips, she forgot the difficulties they faced. She forgot everything except the way it felt to kiss this amazing woman, to touch her and give her as much pleasure as she'd given Nicole.

She pushed her hand between Fiona's trim thighs, finding her as wet as Nicole was. As waves lapped at their ankles and the sun blazed overhead, they touched each other, hips rocking together as their mouths met in an endless kiss. She moaned into Fiona's mouth as she felt herself starting to come. Fiona curled her fingers forward, pressing into that magic spot that sent Nicole right over the edge.

Her hand grew erratic, fingers stroking in and out of Fiona's body as the orgasm rushed through her, crashing over her like a wave that left her weightless and tingly, as if all the cells in her body had turned to glitter. She steadied her breathing, focusing her attention on Fiona, stroking her until her body tensed and her head fell forward onto Nicole's shoulder as she came with a muffled cry.

Then Nicole wrapped her arms around her and held her close. Tears pricked her eyes, and she didn't even know why. She'd found this incredible person who made her feel like no one else ever had before, who made her brave and fearless and even a bit reckless. She felt empowered and strong, more confident than she could ever remember feeling.

But what would happen after they went home?

Fiona lifted her head, her eyes the color of the beach— turquoise waves crashing into the golden sand that ringed her pupils.

"So beautiful," Nicole whispered, hands clutching Fiona's hips, not wanting to let her go. Not now, not ever.

"Shush." Fiona kissed the corner of her mouth.

"We'll see each other again, right?"

Fiona's brow furrowed. "What?"

"After we've been rescued...once we're home."

Fiona looked away, her gaze fixed on some nonexistent entity on the horizon.

"You like your space," Nicole said, hearing the desperation in her voice but not much caring. "So a long-distance relationship could be perfect, really. I could visit—"

"Stop." Fiona cut her off. "It wouldn't work that way, and you know it."

"I know I can't walk away," she said fiercely, foolishly. "I know I can't say goodbye."

"You're going through a divorce. You came on this trip to find yourself, but instead, you found me." Fiona shook her head. "You still need to do the other part...and you have to do it without me."

"No." She swiped at the tears spilling over her lids, but she heard the truth in Fiona's words, much as she hated it. She *did* need to find her footing in her post-divorce life, but there had to be a way to do it without saying goodbye.

She was falling for Fiona, and she was worried sick about her health. Everything seemed to be unraveling around them, and Nicole had no idea how to fix it.

"Friends," Fiona said with a slightly pained smile. "We'll stay friends."

"Are you serious?" Nicole drew back, staring at her.

"Yes."

"That's bullshit, Fi. Friends?"

Fiona's jaw clenched, her gaze locked stubbornly on the ocean. "Would you rather we cut ties entirely?"

"I'd rather we not end things at all."

"I told you that night on the *Cyprus Star*." Fiona's voice had gone hoarse. "I don't have relationships like this."

"Just sex, right?" Nicole didn't even try to keep the accusation out of her tone.

"That's right." Fiona stared blankly at the horizon.

"Look me in the goddamn eyes and tell me this is just sex."

Fiona's eyes flicked to hers, something unspeakably sad in their blue depths. "It's not just sex, but don't make it more than it is either."

"I'm not making it anything," Nicole said, swallowing past the pain in her throat. "I just don't want to decide ahead of time that it has to end when we go home."

Fiona walked past her, headed toward their campsite. "Fine, then. We'll talk about it once we're rescued."

9

Nicole whooped as she yanked the line, lifting a yellow-striped fish out of the water. It was about damn time, but she'd caught three fish now and had decided to keep going despite her fatigue. She'd catch them a feast to celebrate their successful relocation down the beach.

She turned and carried this one to shore, laying it next to the other two on a flat rock she'd placed there for this purpose. She picked up the fishing knife and inserted it into the fish's belly, slicing it open. This being her third attempt, she'd gotten better at it, and removed the fish's guts with some finesse, then brought all the yuck with her back to the water to use as bait.

About ten feet away, Fiona sat on a rock beside their new fire. It had taken most of the day to get here. They'd filled two thermal suits with supplies and carried them down the beach, their progress hampered by the awkward packs they carried.

Fiona hadn't complained, but Nicole saw her struggling more than usual. She'd gotten quieter as the day wore on, hadn't protested when Nicole suggested she stay and get their new fire going while Nicole made the return trip to bring a second round of supplies. The area around her wound was even more red and swollen, and it continued to drain down her leg. If it got much worse, they might have to take their chances in the lifeboat, because Fiona needed to get to a hospital, and soon.

Neither of them had mentioned their argument that morning. Fiona seemed determined to avoid the topic, and with her health worsening, Nicole had decided to let it slide until after they were rescued. But once they were safe? Oh, they were definitely having that conversation.

She returned to the water to keep fishing. The beach here was open and wide, allowing them a full one-hundred-and-eighty-degree view of the sea beyond. If anyone was out there looking for them, they should be easier to find here than they had been at their first beach. They'd fashioned a new SOS sign in the sand and hoped the smoke from their fire served as another beacon to their whereabouts.

Behind her, Fiona strung the fish on a stick and carried them to the fire. Soon, the smell of roasting fish filled the air, and Nicole's stomach rumbled loudly. She reeled in a fourth fish and then a fifth.

"I think you've caught enough," Fiona said as she poked fish onto a second stick.

"They're not very big, but yeah, this is probably enough. I'm so hungry, though."

"This is plenty," Fiona insisted, indicating that Nicole should sit beside her on the rock. "You haven't sat down all day. Come and rest a bit."

It was true. Nicole had been on a mission today: get all the things done. Now that she sat, she felt weary to her bones. It was a good kind of weary, though. She'd actually gotten all the things done, or most of them anyway. They were in much better shape tonight than they had been last night, with the exception of Fiona's leg.

They hadn't located a source of fresh water yet, but hopefully, they wouldn't be here long enough for it to become a problem. She leaned into Fiona, then pressed a hand against her shoulder. "Did you get sunburned today?"

"Maybe a little. Why?"

"Your skin is so hot."

"Mm," Fiona said with a shrug. "I'll have to be better with the sun cape tomorrow."

"You don't look red."

"The sun is getting low." Fiona leaned forward, adjusting the fish on their makeshift spit.

Nicole touched her thigh, felt the heat radiating off her. "You're running a fever."

"Probably just a sunburn like you said."

Nicole blinked back tears. "Maybe."

It was a fever, and they both knew it. The infection was getting worse. She wanted to hand Fiona a packet of aspirin. She must feel awful. But maybe it was better to let her body wage this battle without attempting to tame it. Maybe the fever would win against the infection. So she didn't offer, and Fiona didn't ask.

She sipped from the water Nicole offered and picked at the fish once they were finished cooking. Nicole demolished three of them and could have eaten more, but she insisted Fiona eat the other two, even though she looked like she would rather have stopped after the first one. Fever or not, she needed to eat to keep up her strength.

After they'd cleaned up their supper and washed off in the surf, Nicole got the flashlight to tend to Fiona's wound one more time before bed. She dabbed at it with an antiseptic wipe. At this point, she knew it wasn't doing much—if any—good, but it still felt better than doing nothing. Under the glare of the flashlight, a red line was visible, extending from the edge of the wound about halfway up Fiona's inner thigh.

Nicole's breath hitched, and panic clutched at her stomach. *Oh God.* Had the infection spread to her bloodstream? Their situation had just gone from bad to dire, and Nicole's brain was spinning on the implications.

"What?" Fiona asked.

Nicole schooled her expression. "It looks a little worse, that's all."

She turned off the flashlight and put away the first aid kit. Fiona didn't ask for details. Maybe she didn't want to know. Maybe it was better for her not to. Together, they climbed the hill to the ruins where they'd first had sex, their new home away from home. Earlier, Nicole had laid their sleeping sacks here, spread out like a blanket the way Fiona had prepared them last night.

They lay together, facing each other and hands entwined. Fiona's eyes were bright with fever, her brow knitted with pain.

"I'm sorry," Nicole whispered, pulling her close.

"It'll be better in the morning." Fiona rolled away, scooting toward her so they were spooned together, her back to Nicole's front.

Nicole wrapped an arm around her, hoping her words were true. She lay there for a long time, hoping, as the last glimmer of the sun faded away and the moon rose bright and silvery over the sea. Fiona's breathing evened out as she drifted into sleep, but it was a restless sleep. She tossed and thrashed, occasionally mumbling and whimpering under her breath. Sweat slicked her skin.

Nicole rubbed a hand up and down her back, feeling the danger of their situation more acutely than ever. Until now, logic had dictated that their best hope of rescue was to stay on the island and make themselves as visible as possible. Fishermen were sure to find them sooner or later.

Venturing out again in the lifeboat had a high risk of failure. They had no fuel and were running low on water. They might float safely to the mainland, or they might drift helplessly out to sea. But if they stayed here on the island another day, Fiona might die, so Nicole didn't see that they had a choice.

Tomorrow, it would be time to take matters into their own hands and save themselves.

PAIN. So much pain. Everything hurt, from her scalp to her toes, centered in the endless throbbing that radiated from the wound on her leg. Sometime during the night, Fiona slipped out of bed, carefully disentangling herself from the arm Nicole had wrapped around her. She walked to the edge of the pavilion and stood looking down at the beach.

Not that she could see the ocean, but she could hear it. The moon had sunk below the horizon hours ago, leaving them in total darkness. Above, the heavens glowed with endless stars, a fact she would have appreciated a lot more if her eyes would focus properly.

It would be foolish to stumble around in the dark when she was semi-delirious, so instead she sat at the edge of the pavilion, resting her cheek against the cool marble of the nearest column. Her throat was parched, but she couldn't remember where they'd left their water supply after their relocation and probably shouldn't drink anything anyway.

Not only were they running low on water, but her stomach felt queasy enough that she'd probably throw up if she tried to put anything in it.

She had no idea how long she'd been sitting there before she felt movement behind her. Nicole's hand landed on her shoulder, and Fiona leaned unconsciously into her touch, helpless to fight the pull of the connection that ran between them.

"You okay?" Nicole asked softly.

"Couldn't sleep."

"Need anything?"

She shook her head against Nicole's shoulder. "Talking to you is nice, though."

"Your fever's worse."

She didn't answer, didn't have to when they both already knew the truth.

"When the sun rises, I'm going to pack the lifeboat. If we're lucky, the tide will carry us to safety before nightfall."

"Or it will suck us back out to sea." But she didn't have the strength to launch a proper argument against Nicole's flawed logic. Maybe her own logic was just as flawed. Her brain felt like it had been stuffed with cotton and lit on fire.

"I think we need to take our chances."

Fiona was quiet. The thought of getting back on that boat—especially when she felt like this—was almost too much. But they hadn't gotten this far by backing down when things got tough.

"I'm turning forty in a few months," she said instead.

"What?"

Yeah, Fiona wasn't sure where that had come from either. Her brain wasn't quite in line with her mouth tonight. "It's been on my mind these last few days, that's all."

"You'll be home long before then," Nicole said, giving her a squeeze.

Will I? Fiona had never considered the possibility that she wouldn't survive this. But sitting here racked with fever, infection raging, she wondered. "Not a big deal," she mumbled. "Just a number."

"Does that mean you don't want me to get you one of those Forty and Fabulous shirts?" Nicole asked, nudging her gently.

"Don't you dare," she whispered, a smile tugging at her lips.

"You'll be home, Fi," Nicole said again, stronger this time. "Telling stories about our adventure to all your friends."

"Pfft." Fiona dropped her head against Nicole's shoulder. "Celebrating alone."

"I may fight you on that part."

"I'll win." She sucked in a breath as a particularly vicious bolt of pain radiated through her.

Nicole held on to her as the night wore on. Fiona didn't feel herself shaking until her knees started knocking together. At some point, Nicole fell asleep, slumped against her. The steady rhythm of her breathing was soothing. Fiona wanted to close her eyes and sleep for a million years, but her body wouldn't cooperate.

It hurt and burned and shook until she was ready to scream in frustration. Her fingers clenched around the edge of the pavilion, her head bowed in exhaustion. Sweat ran like a river down her back, puddling in the fabric of her skirt.

When she lifted her head, a glimmer of light caught her eye. Not their campfire, still flickering on the beach. Not the stars or the moon. This was brighter, a cluster of lights in the darkened expanse of the sea.

A boat.

It had to be a boat. Or was she hallucinating? She might be hallucinating. She blinked hard, staring into the enveloping blackness of the night. The lights swam before her eyes, fading in and out, and she had no idea whether they were real or a product of her fevered state.

"Nicole," she whispered, nudging her awake.

Nicole lurched upright, nearly tumbling off the edge of the pavilion. Fiona wrapped a hand around her biceps, anchoring them against each other. "Mm," Nicole mumbled. "You okay?"

"Look," she said by way of an answer. If the boat was real, Nicole would see it.

Nicole was silent for a long moment, so long that Fiona decided there was nothing to see after all. Nicole was squinting into the darkness and wondering what the hell she was supposed to be looking at.

"Oh my God," she whispered finally, her hand clamping around Fiona's. "It's a boat, and it looks big...and close."

Then they were both up and running, scrambling through the scrubby terrain to the bag on the beach where they'd left their supplies. Nicole clicked on the flashlight and rummaged around, coming up with their last remaining flare.

Fiona's toes dug into the sand as her vision tunneled and her knees turned to water. She gripped Nicole to keep herself upright. Nicole held on to her with one hand while with the other, she lifted the flare overhead and fired.

10

Nicole would remember the next few hours as a dizzying blur punctuated by brief flashes of clarity. The moment the boat had definitively turned toward them. The initial shouts of the fishermen as they approached the shore. The horrifying moment when Fiona fell to the sand, eyes rolling back in her head.

The fishermen took them swiftly onto their boat—a Greek fishing vessel, as it turned out—and headed immediately for the mainland. They settled Fiona into one of their bunks, plying them both with food and water, although Nicole was too worried to eat, and Fiona was too sick. She seemed somewhat revived by their rescue, though, and conversed briefly with the fishermen in their own language.

"You speak Greek?" Nicole asked once they'd been left alone. The sleeping compartment was cramped and smelled strongly of fish. She wished she'd thought to grab her clothes before they left the island, but here she was, on a boat full of men, wearing only a few scraps of red fabric. Fiona at least had a sheet thrown over her.

"A little," she answered with a wan smile. "I understand it better than I speak it. My, ah, friend is Greek."

"The one who stood you up?"

"Yes."

Fuck it. Nicole stood and grabbed a sheet off one of the other bunks, wrapping it around herself so she didn't flash the next person to enter the room.

"He said the authorities boarded the *Cyprus Star* yesterday. They rescued the remaining hostages, although many had been killed."

Nicole inhaled roughly. "Oh my God."

"I know." Fiona closed her eyes and swallowed, hard. "It smells awful in here."

"It does." Nicole laughed in spite of herself. "Please don't puke in their bunk."

"Trying not to." Fiona took several long, deep breaths, pain etched into the deep creases in her brow. "He said an alert went out yesterday to be on the lookout for us. They had already pulled closer to the island because of our fire. When they saw the flare, they knew they'd found us."

"Wow." Nicole blew out a breath as emotion rolled over her in a tidal wave. People had died onboard the *Cyprus Star*. If not for sheer luck and Fiona's quick thinking, she and Fiona might have been among them. Instead, they were safe. They were going home. Fiona would surely be okay now that they were on their way to the hospital, although the fear knotting Nicole's gut wouldn't ease until they got there and a doctor told her it was true.

She slid out of her chair and knelt on the floor beside Fiona. Nicole wrapped her arms around her and wept. Fiona was still, silent, but when her eyes met Nicole's, her face was streaked with tears.

FIONA LINGERED SOMEWHERE between pain and relief and the fear that none of this was actually happening. It was all an elaborate fever dream, and she'd jerk awake at any moment to find herself back on the island with Nicole. Not that sleeping with Nicole beneath the stars was a hardship...

Her eyes snapped open, and she lurched upright, chest heaving, body soaked in sweat.

"Shh," Nicole murmured from beside her. "It was just a dream."

"What?" Panic raced through her, flooding her body with adrenaline. A dream? No. As her eyes blinked into focus, she saw the green gown on her body, heard the beeping of medical equipment, smelled the antiseptic scent of a hospital.

"We're safe," Nicole said, one arm wrapped around Fiona's stomach. "You had a bad dream, but we're safe."

"Safe," she repeated, slumping back against the sheets.

"Mm-hmm." Nicole nuzzled her neck. "Remember the fishing boat? The stinky bunkroom?"

Fiona smiled. "Yeah."

And now that her brain had caught up to speed, she remembered arriving at the hospital too. They'd cleaned and flushed her wound, bandaged it, and hooked her up to an IV full of antibiotics.

"How do you feel?" Nicole asked.

"Better." She rolled cautiously onto her side, careful not to disturb the tube in her arm. "I think they gave me some good drugs. How long was I asleep?"

"A few hours, I think. I slept too."

"Why are you here?"

Nicole made a noise of disbelief. "Where else would I be?"

"Are you hurt?" She raised her head and peered at Nicole. She wore an oversized blue T-shirt, black leggings, and an incredulous smile.

"I'm perfectly fine, and I'm not leaving your side."

"Stop it." Fiona turned her face toward the pillow in a pathetic attempt to hide the tears on her face and the catch in her voice.

"You stop it," Nicole countered, drawing Fiona's head against her chest. "You scared the shit out of me last night— this morning—whatever time it was when we were rescued. I swear to God, your face was so pale, you turned green, and then you collapsed in the sand..."

"Well, I'm feeling much better now," Fiona said, forcing some strength into her voice.

"Amazing what a few hours of antibiotics will do, isn't it?"

"Yes." Fiona pushed herself up to a sitting position and reached for the pitcher of water on a tray beside her bed. Her throat was so dry, it felt scorched.

Nicole reached past her and poured her a glass, which was probably for the best because Fiona's hands shook violently when she lifted the cup toward her mouth. Nicole steadied it for her. "You were dehydrated," she said.

Fiona drained the glass. "Not anymore."

"I should have made you drink more water when your fever spiked. Everyone knows—"

Fiona silenced her with a kiss. "Don't do that. You took great care of me, even when I was a total pain in the ass."

Nicole grinned at her. "You were never a pain in the ass."

"I'm always a pain in the ass."

"Is there anything else you need? What can I get you?"

Fiona looked at the IV stand beside her bed. "Can I walk with this thing?"

"Yes. You were pretty out of it earlier, so they showed me instead." Nicole slid out of bed and walked to the stand. She lifted the IV bag from the pole attached to the bed to the portable stand, then pushed a lever at the base and rolled it back and forth. "Okay. I think you're good to go."

"Thank you." Fiona took the hand she offered and stood on shaky legs. Feeling like an eighty-year-old woman, she shuffled toward the bathroom. A draft of air drifted across her backside. Fucking hospital gowns. "I know you're staring at my ass," she called over her shoulder as she pushed the IV stand into the bathroom.

"News flash. I've been staring at your ass for the better part of a week now," Nicole shot back.

Fiona managed to get in and out of the bathroom without further incident, holding in a groan as she climbed back into bed. She felt a hundred times better than she had last night on the island, but her whole body still hurt all the way to her bones. "Who do I see about getting out of here?"

"Three days of IV antibiotics. That's what they said," Nicole told her gravely.

Fiona felt her jaw jutting automatically in defiance. She desperately needed to get out of here, to go somewhere quiet where she could recuperate in peace. "Three days?"

Nicole gave her a sympathetic look. "It sucks, but you're still sick."

"I'd feel so much better if I could go home," she muttered, unable to keep the bitterness out of her tone. Three days in the hospital sounded like an eternity. On the island, she'd been able to find peace and quiet when she needed it. Here, she'd have nothing but beeping machines, open-backed gowns, and nurses fussing over her.

"At least you get a real bed to sleep in tonight, even if it's a hospital bed."

"Mm." She rolled toward Nicole, wrapping an arm around her. "And where will you be sleeping tonight?"

"Right here with you."

"You don't have to, you know. You should go to a hotel, take a long bath, live it up."

"I've already used your shower, and the hospital staff hooked me up with some clothes that…well, I'm not sure if I want to know where they came from, but they're clean. I guess they're bringing our suitcases to us." Nicole's brow furrowed. "The police want to talk to us, and apparently, the press is camped outside, hoping to interview us. Oh, and my parents are on their way."

Fiona stiffened. "Your parents?"

"They flew to Italy when they found out the *Cyprus Star* had been hijacked, and they're on their way here to Greece now."

Fiona's stomach soured. "You'll go when they get here, then?"

"I told them to come here."

"To my hospital room?" Fiona's voice had risen to a pitch she didn't even recognize.

"To the hospital, yes. They're very nice. They want to meet you." Nicole paused, her expression heartbreakingly earnest. "You'll like them."

I don't like anyone, Fiona wanted to say. "What did you tell them?" she said instead.

Nicole ducked her head. "About us? Nothing really. I mean, they're Italian, so they both talk a lot, and they were so worried…I hardly got a word in edgewise."

Fiona turned away as tension snaked through her body.

"I'd rather be alone. You should go with them when they get here."

Nicole's hand found hers under the sheet. "How many times do I have to say *I'm not leaving you* before it sinks into your stubborn head?"

She turned her gaze toward the window, jaw set, skin prickling.

"I didn't think I should say anything about our relationship to anyone just yet," Nicole said softly, mistaking the cause of Fiona's discomfort. "I mean, I thought we should figure it out together first."

"I've already told you what's going to happen." Fiona's voice had gone hoarse, and she reached over to pour herself another glass of water, relieved to find her hands steadier now.

"When you get out of the hospital, we'll go to the hotel...*together*, and we'll talk about it then. Until then, you're stuck with me." Nicole tugged at her hand, and Fiona turned toward her. "As long as you don't mind?"

"I don't mind," Fiona whispered, defenses crumbling beneath Nicole's warm eyes and soft heart, the heat of her fingers and the strength of her embrace. Fiona settled onto the sheet beside her, bringing her lips to Nicole's.

Nicole's kiss grounded her. She was safe here in this bed, in Nicole's arms, tethered to life by this incredible person she would never even have dreamed of meeting a week ago. She held on to her with both hands, tears on her cheeks and an avalanche of emotion tearing through her mind. They'd both be on their way home soon enough, Nicole to New York and Fiona to France. Until then, she couldn't bring herself to let her go. "Stay."

11

They ate hospital food together on the tray over Fiona's bed—fish and mixed vegetables with bread and some kind of pudding in little cups. Nicole thought it was one of the best meals she'd ever eaten, although she was probably just starved for real food. Fiona grumbled about hating seafood, only picking at her meal, but she was still feverish, which was probably the real reason she wasn't hungry.

The nurses seemed pleased with her response to the antibiotics, though, so Nicole was finally able to stop worrying about her. Fiona was going to be okay. They were really and truly safe.

They laughed as they ate, wiggling their toes together beneath the sheets, and Nicole felt happier than she could remember feeling pretty much...ever. She knew she had some stuff to sort out and that Fiona had demons of her own, but she was determined to keep this connection between them. It was way too important to risk losing. After lunch, a nurse came in to check on Fiona and showed Nicole how to help her take a shower.

"I feel so much better," Fiona said as she crawled back into bed, fresh and clean, her hair hanging long and wet down her back.

Nicole settled next to her with a smile. "Good enough to turn forty?"

Fiona scrunched her nose. "Did I really blubber about that last night?"

Nicole couldn't contain her laugh. "You did. So when's the big day?"

"Not until September, and it's not a big day. I have no idea why I even mentioned it." She turned her face toward the ceiling.

Nicole wrapped an arm around her. "You were scared."

"I was delirious."

"Maybe a little of both." Nicole gave her a gentle squeeze. She was exhausted, and Fiona must be even more so. They fell asleep together, arms around each other, holding on for dear life.

A knock at the door startled Nicole awake. Fiona blinked at her, blue eyes bleary but clear, alert. Her skin felt cool. Her fever had broken. It was amazing how quickly the antibiotics had kicked in, and Nicole was so thankful for it, she could cry.

A frown tugged at Fiona's lips as she turned her head toward the door. "Come in."

It pushed open, and Nicole's parents entered the room, and *oh my God*, she'd almost forgotten they were on their way. She really had meant to offer to keep them out of Fiona's room. Now that they were here and she saw the tense, guarded expression in Fiona's eyes, she wished she had.

Nicole pushed herself quickly out of bed. "Mom, Dad..." Tears spilled over her eyelids as she rushed toward them, as if the sight of them had triggered the emotions she'd worked so hard to hold at bay the whole time they were lost, the fear that they wouldn't get home, that she'd never see her family again, that they'd have to bury her or, worse, live the rest of their lives never knowing what had happened to her. "It's so good to see you."

In response, her mother burst into tears, clutching Nicole against her chest while her father stood there, nervously stroking her hair. "We were so worried," her mom sobbed.

"I know." She gulped, trying to pull herself back together.

"I can't even imagine what you've been through," her dad said, abandoning all pretense of restraint and joining in the hug.

"First, they told us your boat had been taken hostage, and then they told us you weren't even on it...that you were somehow lost at sea..." Another sob racked her mother.

"It's been, well, it was quite an adventure anyway." Nicole glanced over at Fiona, saw her sitting there alone in bed, arms crossed over her chest, eyes deliberately cast toward the window, and her chest caved in on itself. Was anyone going to come here to visit her? Would her father?

Nicole's mom followed her gaze, turning toward Fiona. She wiped the tears from her face and smiled. "And you must be Fiona. I'm Michelle, Nicole's mom, and this is my husband, Anthony."

"Hello," Fiona said politely, a warm—if slightly stiff—smile on her face.

But Nicole's mom was already closing in on her, pulling her in for a hug, and Fiona's eyes went comically round as they met Nicole's from across the room.

"She's British, Mom," Nicole said with a laugh. "They don't really hug like we do, I don't think."

"Everyone needs a hug after going through an ordeal like this," Michelle said, releasing Fiona, who slumped back in bed, her cheeks suspiciously pink.

Nicole retreated to the bed and sat beside her, sliding her hand into Fiona's. And that was when it hit her, the difference between dating a man and a woman. Nicole's parents had just walked in on her and Fiona in bed together, saw them now holding hands, and thought absolutely nothing of it simply because Fiona was female.

Well, she'd have that conversation with them later, because no matter how things played out with Fiona, Nicole was going to embrace her sexuality from here on out.

Her parents sat on either side of the bed, and she and Fiona gave them the sex-free version of the events that had unfolded over the past week, while her mom and dad gasped and cried and freaked out all over again knowing just what exactly she'd been through.

Naturally, they'd brought food—fresh pizzelle from a stand in Italy. The Italian waffle cookies were one of Nicole's top favorite foods, and these were possibly the best ones she'd ever tasted. "These are so freaking good," she said around a mouthful, drawing an amused glance from Fiona, who ate hers much more delicately.

"I know they're your favorite," Michelle said. "As soon as we heard you'd been found, we booked the first flight to Greece, and then I found a place to stop and buy these for you."

"Reasons why you're the best mom on the planet." Nicole leaned over to plant a kiss on her mother's cheek.

"When are they letting you out of here?" her dad asked.

"I'm not *in* here," Nicole said. "But Fiona has to stay a few days, and I'm staying with her."

"That's so sweet," her mom said. "You two really bonded out there, didn't you?"

Fiona lowered her eyes, wiping at a pizzella crumb on her cheek.

"Yeah, we did." Nicole reached for her hand and gave it another squeeze.

"Being lost at sea like that, I can't even imagine." Michelle shook her head. "You look exhausted, sweetie," she said to Fiona.

"I'm fine," Fiona said, but the dark smudges under her eyes told a different story.

"Twelve hours ago, she was so sick, she collapsed on the beach," Nicole said. "Scared the life out of me."

Fiona chewed her lip, clearly uncomfortable with the shift in the conversation.

Michelle patted her hand. "We should let you rest."

"You should go with them," Fiona said, giving Nicole a meaningful look. "Go out for a bit. I could use a nap, like she said."

"Well..." Nicole's instinct was to reject the idea. She didn't want to leave Fiona even for a minute, but she knew having her parents here was probably exhausting and over-whelming for her. She *did* need to rest. "Okay, but I'll be back soon."

"Take your time. Really."

"We'll find someplace to have an early supper," her dad suggested.

"And we can get you girls some clothes and supplies, whatever you need," her mom added.

"Supposedly, our suitcases are being returned to us in

the morning," Nicole said. "But a few supplies couldn't hurt. Oh, and Fi, we can get you a new cell phone."

Fiona brightened at the idea. "That would be fantastic, actually."

"Perfect," Michelle said. "We'll bring you back some supper too, something better than hospital food." She winked conspiratorially.

Fiona ducked her head with a shy smile. "Thank you."

There was another knock at the door, and everyone's heads swiveled toward it in unison.

"Come in," Fiona called.

Nicole turned toward her mom to ask her what hotel they were staying in, assuming one of the nurses had come to check on Fiona, but a tall, gray-haired man stepped into the room instead. Fiona let out a small sound, as if someone had just sat on her chest, forcing the air from her lungs. Nicole took one look between them before her brain caught up to speed.

Fiona's dad had come after all. And she didn't look happy about it. She sat frozen in bed, eyes locked on the man in the doorway, her cheeks as pale as they'd been this morning on the beach right before she crumpled onto the sand. Instinctively, Nicole inched closer, allowing her shoulder to bump into Fiona's, offering her silent support.

Michelle turned toward him with a warm smile. "Hello. Are you Fiona's dad?"

He cleared his throat. "I am, yes. Oliver Boone." He spoke in a clipped British accent. His white button-down shirt was neatly pressed; his gray pants almost an exact match for his eyes. If he was worried about what Fiona had been through, he didn't show it, but then again, maybe British people weren't as expressive as Americans that way.

"Michelle Morella," Nicole's mom said, standing and

extending her hand. "And this is my husband, Anthony. We're Nicole's parents," she explained, as if this man knew who Nicole was. Did he? Had Fiona called him, or had he come of his own accord?

Fiona hadn't spoken, hadn't moved, maybe hadn't even breathed since he entered the room, and Nicole felt helpless, unsure what to do or say to make this any easier for her. The silence stretched to a length that became uncomfortable, and Nicole's dad got up from his chair.

"We'll just give you guys a few minutes to catch up," he said.

Her mom followed. "We'll be in the hall. Help yourselves to the pizzelle."

Nicole glanced over at Fiona, unsure whether to stay or go.

"Go," Fiona muttered. Her father lingered in the doorway, jacket folded neatly over one arm. "It's fine," she insisted when Nicole hesitated.

"Okay, but I'll be right outside." Nicole had to resist the urge to kiss her before she slid out of bed, but she wasn't completely sure whether Fiona was out to her family, and she was completely sure Fiona would hate being kissed in front of her father regardless.

With one last glance over her shoulder, Nicole stepped into the hall. Her parents stood staring at her with matching uncomfortable expressions.

"What was that about?" her mom asked.

"British people aren't *that* stiff around each other, are they?" her dad chimed in.

She shook her head. "No, it's... They aren't close. I don't know the history."

"That's sad," her mom said. "But while I've got you out here, tell me, are you really okay?"

"I really am, Mom." Nicole let her mother fold her into another hug. "That lifeboat was crazy well stocked. We had pretty much everything we needed...except antibiotics for Fiona."

"How did she cut her leg?" her dad asked.

"Scaling the side of the ship to pull the safety pins that released the lifeboat." Nicole laughed at the expressions on her parents' faces. "I know it sounds crazy. It *was* crazy. We could have died at least a hundred different ways, and yet here I am, with hardly a scratch on me."

Nicole had gotten off easy. Fiona had suffered so much more. She was in there right now, facing her estranged father all by herself, and there wasn't a damn thing Nicole could do to make it any easier for her.

FIONA STARED AT HER HANDS, noting every scratch that marred her skin, her chipped nails, the heart rate monitor strapped to her index finger, and the IV taped to the back of her right hand. She needed her beeswax moisturizing cream. It might help smooth over some of her rough edges.

Her father cleared his throat. "It's a relief to know you're safe."

She nodded, her throat as parched as it had been when she first arrived at the hospital. He stood by the window, so tall and imposing, every stitch of his clothing neatly pressed. By comparison, she felt small and rumpled, unable to even stand and face him without exposing her bare ass in the hospital gown.

"The authorities kept me apprised of your situation," he said. "I was quite beside myself with worry."

"I'm sorry I didn't call," she managed. Her mind was

replaying the previous reunion in this room, the way the Morellas had hugged and cried, shared food and laughter as Nicole filled them in on everything that had happened. Fiona and her father could barely look at each other.

"Don't be," he said. "You've had enough to deal with. I came expecting...well, I wasn't sure what to expect."

"I'm fine." She picked at a broken fingernail until it splintered, a crimson droplet of blood swelling on her fingertip. Embarrassed, she snatched a tissue from the box beside her bed and wrapped it around her finger.

Her father took a step closer to the bed. "I spent a lot of time thinking this week."

She gazed resolutely at her lap. The beeping of her heart rate on the machine quickened, obnoxious to the point that she almost slipped the monitor off her finger to silence it.

"I have so many regrets," he said quietly.

"Don't," she warned as the tissue shredded between her fingers. "Not today."

Her father nodded. "Perhaps you'd like to come home for a bit after you're released?"

"No." It came out harsher than she'd intended. "Thank you."

"Another time, then," he said, turning away. "It's good to see you, Fiona. I'm glad you're okay."

She wasn't okay. She was so far from okay. She clenched her fingers, wishing like hell she wasn't trapped in this fucking hospital bed. "Thank you for coming."

"Take care," he said before stepping back into the hallway.

The door closed behind him with a soft click. She lay back in bed and squeezed her eyes shut, sucking in a deep breath and pushing it out from her diaphragm, one after another until the beeping of the machine returned to normal.

The door clicked again, and light footsteps approached the bed. "You okay?"

It was Nicole.

Fiona opened her eyes slowly, tucking her hand beneath the sheet to hide her bloody fingernail and the shredded tissue. "Fine. Just tired."

"How'd it go with your dad?"

"Fine," she repeated, putting as much weight into the word as she could muster.

"I'll let you sleep, then," Nicole said, leaning in to kiss her cheek. "We'll be back later with food and stuff."

"Thank you," she whispered, turning away.

She waited until Nicole had left the room before letting the tears fall. Alone. Finally. The peace and quiet she'd been yearning for. She fought against the irrational urge to get up and lock the door. The beeping of the machine spiked again.

Her father had regrets? Well, so did she. Seeing him today was a timely reminder that the only person she had ever really been able to count on was herself.

A nurse came into the room, bustling over to her bed and ending Fiona's brief time alone. She looked at the heart rate machine and then at Fiona. "Too many guests, yes?" she said in a heavy Greek accent.

Fiona nodded.

"You want something to help you sleep?"

She hesitated for a moment, but sleep would be her only respite until she got out of this place, and her brain was too wired right now to come by it naturally. "Please."

The nurse left, returning a few minutes later with a small paper cup containing a white pill. She poured a glass of water and handed them both to Fiona. "I keep everyone out for you while you rest."

"Thank you." She swallowed the pill, ridiculously grateful for the promise of solitude and sleep.

The nurse checked her over, then closed the blinds on her window, turned out the light, and headed for the door.

"Wait," Fiona called.

The nurse paused in the doorway, looking back at her.

"My friend Nicole," she said, twisting her fingers beneath the sheet. "You can let her in...if she comes back."

The nurse nodded with a knowing smile. "She will be back."

12

F iona couldn't contain the sigh of relief that escaped her lips as she stepped inside her hotel room. It was big and shiny and expensive looking, the kind of place she never booked for herself but never minded when someone else did. In this case, it was a gesture of goodwill from the *Cyprus Star*'s parent company. The cruise line had been in touch with both her and Nicole, hoping to win back their good graces.

"This is...fancy," Nicole said from behind her.

"It is. I bet it has a lovely tub." Fiona kicked the door shut behind them, trying not to let on how exhausted she was from spending the evening with Nicole and her parents. She'd hardly done anything but sleep in the days since their rescue, and yet she still felt tired and weak. It was beyond frustrating.

In the end, she'd sweet-talked the doctors into letting her out after only two nights, and she was so grateful, she could cry. Between the doctors, nurses, Nicole, and her parents constantly bustling in and out of her room, Fiona had exceeded her capacity for human interaction. She was desperate for quiet, for a hot bath and a soft bed...the things she'd been longing for since their time on the island.

The whole time she was hospitalized, Nicole had looked so damn happy that Fiona couldn't even be annoyed with her for letting her parents invade her room. They were lovely people. It wasn't their fault Fiona was terminally anti-social. Nicole had spent both nights in Fiona's hospital bed, as promised, and most of today too. Fiona hadn't been released until half past three this afternoon, and the Morellas had promptly taken them both out to dinner.

Now all she really wanted to do was fall face-first into bed, but she was determined to properly enjoy her last night with Nicole.

"At long last, we've found the resort just over the hill," Nicole said with a quiet laugh.

"Don't you want to see your own room?" Fiona asked teasingly.

"Not even the least bit curious," Nicole answered without hesitation. "In fact, I don't plan to set one foot inside it."

"What if I kick you out?"

Nicole narrowed her eyes at her. "In that case, I might go stay with my parents."

"Do you want to be with your parents?" Fiona asked, purposely needling her, but also curious about the kind of warm, affectionate relationship Nicole had with her family, something Fiona had never known.

"Not tonight," Nicole answered, stepping closer and sliding her hands around Fiona's waist.

"But tomorrow?" she pushed.

Nicole let out a frustrated groan. "Yes, tomorrow. They're my parents, but right now, I don't want to talk about them."

"They seem very nice," Fiona said, nuzzling her nose against Nicole's.

"They are, and they like you a lot too." Nicole pressed their lips together. "So, can I stay? Please?"

"Stay." Fiona wrapped her arms around her, pulling her flush against her body. "After all this time, we're finally alone in a hotel room. We've got all the amenities we need. That bed looks really soft. And I want to fuck you in it...repeatedly."

Nicole's eyes had glazed over. "Yes. To all of that. Yes."

Fiona slipped her hands into the back pockets of Nicole's jeans. "Not used to seeing you in so many clothes."

"Same." Nicole tugged at the collar of Fiona's blouse. "I can't quite believe we got our suitcases back after all that."

"A lucky turn of events." She spun them, stepping Nicole toward the bed.

"We've had a lot of those."

"Mm." Fiona pushed her back onto the thick duvet, slipping one of her hands between Nicole's legs. She could feel her heat even through the denim of her jeans. Nicole rolled her hips, taking full advantage of the contact.

Fiona knelt on top of her, wincing as her bandaged shin sank into the mattress, sending a shock wave of pain radiating up her leg. "Dammit."

"You're not good at being injured, are you?" Nicole sat up, rolling Fiona to the bed beside her. "What am I going to have to do to keep you off your knees tonight?"

"Don't make me beg." Fiona tugged at the button on Nicole's jeans. "I might even need your help getting in and out of the tub without getting my leg wet."

"I can definitely help with that," Nicole said, making short work of the buttons on Fiona's blouse. "Although first I want to put my attention toward getting other parts of you wet."

"Too late," Fiona murmured against her neck. "Already wet."

Nicole pushed Fiona's blouse over her shoulders, bending to press hot, openmouthed kisses down her chest to her navel. She tongued the piercing there, and Fiona arched off the bed, yanking at the loose knit skirt she'd worn to avoid aggravating her injury.

They scrambled out of the rest of their clothes and lay side by side on the bed, facing each other, legs entwined, hands roaming, kissing frantically.

"Does it hurt?" Nicole whispered, looking down at the bandage on Fiona's right leg.

"No." She nudged Nicole's left foot with her right to illustrate her point. "Not unless I bump it."

"I'll be careful," Nicole promised, giggling as her legs slid against Fiona's. "This feels different now that we've both shaved."

"The wonders of modern amenities."

"So smooth." Nicole thrust one of her thighs up so that it pressed against Fiona's center, and she rolled her hips, suddenly overwhelmed by the desire raging inside her. She needed the kind of orgasm Nicole delivered so well. She needed to cleanse herself of the stress of the last two days, the pain, the hospital, so many fucking people. She needed to lose herself in the pleasure of Nicole's touch, and she needed it now.

"You promised you wouldn't make me beg."

"And I never break a promise." Nicole's fingers slid between her legs, sending Fiona's brain whirling in mindless pleasure.

Yes. God, yes.

She touched Nicole, giving as good as she received, stroking her toward oblivion as the same pressure built inside her. Their mouths met in a messy kiss, breasts touching, toes bracing against each other as they pressed together, moving as one. Blonde hair mixed with brown before her eyes, like earth meeting sand at the edge of their beach, blending together to form that unique place where she and Nicole existed in their own special world.

Theirs, and only theirs.

I love you. As the orgasm crashed through her, she had to bite her tongue to hold in the words. Tears slipped over her cheeks, and she kept moving, kept stroking Nicole until she'd joined her, hips bucking as she found release.

"It gets better every time," she whispered, arms tight around Fiona.

"You're just that good," she teased, trying to keep things light, to keep the emotions at bay, because this was their last night together. Tomorrow, they would both fly home, leaving Greece and everything that happened here in their past.

"It's not me," Nicole said softly. "Or you. It's just *us*."

"Maybe it's the bed. Or the fact that we have real food in our bellies."

"You didn't eat very much of your supper," Nicole said.

"I wasn't hungry then." She'd been antsy, irritable, so very tired, yearning for the solitude of the hotel room she hadn't yet seen. "I am now."

"For me, or for food?" Nicole asked with a smile.

"Both."

"Tonight, you can have anything you want."

"Good." She gave her a deep, drunken kiss. "First, I want a hot bath. And then I think we should order room service. Maybe champagne."

Nicole gave her a look. "Okay, that you can't have. Antibiotics, remember?"

Fiona sighed. "Right. No alcohol."

"Promise you'll tell me if you're not feeling well?"

"Promise you'll stop asking me that?" Fiona sat up. "Look, I'm taking my antibiotics without you even reminding me." She twisted the cap off the bottle of water beside the bed and swallowed her pill.

Nicole just smiled.

"Ready for a bath?" Fiona asked.

"It sounds heavenly. I think I could bathe a dozen times a day after going a week without."

"It felt like it took hours to get all the sand out of my hair," Fiona said as she led the way into the bathroom.

"It feels good to be civilized again." Nicole sat on the edge of the tub and started the water running. "Look, they've left you some scented soaps."

"Lovely."

"Although I didn't totally hate being uncivilized together." Nicole glanced at Fiona, something heavy in her expression, as if she was holding in words of her own.

"I didn't either." She dipped her fingers into the water swirling at the bottom of the tub. "But I do like being clean."

"And I never want to eat another food cube again."

Fiona laughed, the kind of laugh that vibrated up from the very deepest parts of her, leaving her light and airy, feeling like she could take on the world. "Shall we?"

"You first." Nicole grabbed a towel from the stack on the counter and placed it on the edge of the tub, gesturing for Fiona to rest her leg there.

"Really unfair that I can't take a proper bath." She fake-pouted as she lowered herself into the hot, swirling water.

"God, this feels good. I was fantasizing about this moment the whole time we were on the island."

Nicole slipped in beside her, groaning as she relaxed into the water.

"Do your parents know you're spending the night in my room?"

She made a noise of frustration. "No. And why do you keep bringing up my parents?"

"I'm just curious."

Nicole looked like she was about to say something, then changed her mind. "Can I come visit you sometime?"

Fiona narrowed her eyes at her. "What?"

"After we're home," Nicole said, her eyes pleading. "I can't say goodbye in the morning, Fi. Promise we'll stay in touch."

"We'll stay in touch." She left it at that, because she wasn't very good at these things, at making emotional connections or keeping in touch with people.

"I've never been to France. What's it like?" Nicole bumped her toes against Fiona's, a gentle nudge like her questions, pushing slowly into places Fiona didn't want touched.

"It's beautiful. Quiet. I'll send you a picture."

"I'd rather see it for myself." But she didn't push harder for an invitation, and for that, Fiona was grateful. "Have you visited America before?"

Fiona nodded. "Several times. It's loud and crowded, and the people are quite rude."

"Sounds like you're describing New York."

"I am." Fiona smiled at her. "You live in a horrible city."

"I happen to love it."

"Good for you."

"Well, you're welcome to visit me any time," Nicole said,

her eyes sparkling dangerously. "I'll show you so much art, it'll blow your mind, and then we can rent a car and leave the city. We could drive into the countryside and rent an extravagant hotel room together like this one."

"Perhaps." She settled lower into the water, closing her eyes, wishing desperately to feel like herself, to be rid of the fatigue and weakness that had plagued her since their rescue.

"I know what you need," Nicole said from the other side of the tub.

"What's that?"

"A massage."

She cracked open an eye, peering at Nicole. "Are you offering?"

"I am."

"Are you any good?"

Nicole shrugged, eyes sparkling. "We'll see, won't we?"

Fiona's gaze caught on the bruise on her thigh, faded now to a garish yellow and green, streaked almost like the imprint of a hand on her skin, and her stomach turned so violently, she almost got sick right there in the tub. Suddenly, she couldn't stand the sight of herself. She turned her head toward the door. "This isn't that comfortable with one of my legs stuck up in the air."

"Ready to get out?"

"Yes."

Nicole reached forward and shut off the water, then pulled the drain. She slipped out of the tub and wrapped a towel around herself, bringing another back for Fiona. She extended a hand to help her out of the tub. Fiona managed not to grumble as she stood. The awkward position had left her with a cramp in the back of her right thigh.

Nicole wrapped the towel around her. "You look exhausted."

"Didn't sleep well in the hospital, all those nurses checking on me."

"And you're still recovering," Nicole reminded her. "Let's order room service, and I'll give you that massage."

"In a minute." Fiona shooed her toward the bathroom door. "Order something for us, will you? I'm not picky."

Nicole looked back at her, *are you okay?* so plainly visible in her eyes that Fiona almost laughed at the ridiculousness of it.

"I just need a minute."

"Okay." Nicole leaned in to give her a kiss and closed the bathroom door behind her.

Fiona sat on the mat in front of the bathtub. She folded her legs and rested her hands on her knees, desperate for the peace she'd found so readily even out there on the beach in the middle of nowhere. Tonight, it was nowhere to be found. Tonight, her leg hurt, and her eyes ached, and her heart felt like it needed a few stitches itself.

She was unraveling like the seam at the edge of the towel Nicole had given her. The room blurred around her, and she blinked back the tears swimming across her vision. Not tonight. Not here. Not while Nicole was sitting in the bedroom, waiting for her and wondering what was wrong.

Not a handprint. Nothing's wrong. I'm fine.

Abandoning the pretense of meditation, she climbed slowly to her feet, wincing at the various aches and pains in her body, ignoring the hideous bruise on her skin, and walked to the bedroom. Nicole sat in the middle of the bed, completely naked, room service menu and phone in hand. She looked over her shoulder at Fiona with a wide smile.

"I was indecisive, so I ordered kind of a lot."

"Sounds perfect." She slid into the bed beside Nicole, dropping her towel to the floor as she did so. Nicole lay back, and Fiona settled with her head on her chest. "Thank you."

"Ready for that massage?"

"Not quite yet." Right now, she just wanted to lie here and listen to the steady rhythm of Nicole's heart beating against her ear. Her eyes drifted shut, and the next thing she knew, someone was knocking at their door.

"Stay here," Nicole whispered. She slipped out of bed, tucked a sheet over Fiona, and grabbed a white robe from the closet by the door before she pulled it open. Fiona just lay there and watched her, struggling to keep her eyes open.

"Food," Nicole announced as she rolled a cart toward their bed. "We've got a cheese plate, some kind of Greek meatballs, stuffed grape leaves, baklava for your sweet tooth, and french fries, because...well, I had a craving, and it was on the menu."

"Wow." Fiona shrugged up on her elbows. "That is possibly the most amazing spread I've ever seen. You have weird but amazing taste in food."

Nicole slid two trays onto the bed, and they sat there—naked—and ate all the food. It was the first full, satisfying meal Fiona had eaten since before they set off on their lifeboat adventure, and she felt immensely better afterward.

"You should get some sleep," Nicole murmured, leaning in for a kiss before clearing away the plates from their bed.

"Not until I've enjoyed the rest of this night with you."

Nicole crawled in behind her, brushing the hair off Fiona's shoulder so she could place an openmouthed kiss there. "It's not our last night together. I refuse to believe that."

Fiona rolled to face her. "You have to go home and sort

yourself out. Date. Date women, if you like. But you can't possibly trust anything you think you're feeling for me, not when we met under these circumstances. You're in the middle of a divorce, and we got thrown into a survival situation together. It was crazy, and what we shared was amazing, but now you've got to get back to your real life."

Nicole blinked back tears. "I hear the words you're saying, but I also know what I feel for you, Fi, and I know what we shared is more than just two people turning to each other for comfort during a tough situation."

"It was more than that," Fiona agreed, pulling Nicole closer. "I've never shared anything like this with anyone else, ever, and I probably never will again."

"Then don't throw it away, Fiona, please." Nicole flung her arms around her, burying her face against her neck. Her tears slid over Fiona's skin, hot and wet.

"I'm not throwing anything away. I'm merely stating facts."

"What if..." Nicole looked up at her, hope mixed with the tears in her eyes. "What if I go home and sort myself out, and I still feel the same way about you?"

Fiona looked away. She didn't know what to say or how to feel. *What if?* "Then call me, and we'll see what happens."

NICOLE SLEPT DEEP AND DREAMLESS, drunk on the soft bed beneath her and the warm woman in her arms, safe and whole and on the mend. In the end, Fiona had slept through most of her self-proclaimed last night with Nicole. She'd put on a brave face, but the exhaustion was plain in her eyes. She'd fallen asleep about five minutes into Nicole's massage and hadn't stirred again.

Nicole had lain there for a long time, watching her sleep and worrying what would happen once they left Greece in the morning. Now, morning was here, and it meant a goodbye she didn't want to say. With a sigh, she rolled over, finding the bed empty and cold beside her.

This wasn't entirely surprising, given Fiona's early morning yoga and meditation habit. Nicole wasn't even worried when she looked around the room and found it empty. Fiona had probably gone outside in search of a peaceful place for her morning routine.

But her suitcase was gone. Holy shit, *all* her things were gone.

"No," Nicole whispered. Fiona would never sneak out without saying goodbye. Except with every gulp of air into her lungs, Nicole realized this might be exactly the kind of thing Fiona would do.

"Dammit, Fi." Nicole rolled over, pounding her fists against the pillow until some of her temper had subsided. Her gaze fell on a piece of paper on the table beside the bed. It was larger than standard notebook paper, crisp and unlined, and something was written on it. No, something was *drawn* on it.

Nicole lurched upright, reaching for the paper. It looked like a page out of a sketchbook, and *oh God*, Fiona had drawn them. She'd drawn them together, here in this bed. The sketch was done with some kind of charcoal pencil, Nicole's dark hair fanning over the pillow as Fiona leaned in to press a kiss against her neck, blonde curls spilling everywhere. She'd signed the drawing at the bottom with a simple "xoxo."

"Dammit, Fi," she whispered again, swiping at the tears puddling in her eyes. She wanted to clutch the drawing against her chest and sob, but she didn't want to ruin it, because it was the most beautiful thing she'd ever seen, a perfect rendering of the love they'd shared.

Yes, she loved Fiona. Maybe she couldn't officially say yet that she was *in* love with her. Fiona was right that Nicole needed to get her act together. Everyone knew that rushing straight out of a divorce into a serious relationship was a recipe for disaster, let alone adding in her first real relationship with a woman. But she loved her, and she would always love her, and she would never, ever forget a single moment they'd shared together.

And she'd find a goddamn way to get in touch with her once she got home to New York, because this was unacceptable. She picked up her phone to check the time and saw a text message from an unknown number.

I had an early flight, and I hate goodbyes. ~ Fi

And all the tears Nicole had been holding back flooded forth, streaming down her cheeks in a mixture of hurt and relief and too many other emotions to sort out. She pressed her face against the pillow until she'd gotten herself under control, and then she picked up her phone and started typing.

I hate you for this.

Also, how did you get my number?

Almost immediately, the little dots began to bounce at the bottom of her screen, letting her know that Fiona was typing back.

Please don't. Your mother gave me your number yesterday when I was programming my new phone.

Nicole was so ridiculously happy to be talking to her that she was grinning like an idiot through her tears. Also, she really owed her mom one.

I don't hate you. I should, but I don't.

And I love the drawing so, so much.

The dots started bouncing again. *I hoped you would. I wish I could chat, but my flight is boarding.*

Safe travels. Talk soon?

Yes.

Nicole flopped back on the bed. She had Fiona's number, and that was more than she'd had a few minutes ago. She'd go home and get her shit together, and then she'd fight for this thing between them with every ounce of her being.

But first, she had her own flight to catch. Reluctantly, Nicole got up and showered and packed her things. She checked out of Fiona's room and met her parents in the lobby.

"You okay?" her mom asked.

She bobbed her head. "Just...emotional about everything, I guess."

"Did Fiona already leave?"

"Yeah."

"It must have been hard saying goodbye after everything you've been through together."

"It was." But she was going to get through it. She thought of the drawing tucked safely away inside her suitcase and smiled.

Fiona might want to think she didn't care, but she did. She cared just as much as Nicole did, and they'd sort this thing out. They would.

She and her parents took a taxi to the airport, and Nicole watched the planes soaring overhead, wondering which one of them was currently jetting toward France. Was Fiona already home? It couldn't be a very long flight, certainly much shorter than the one to New York.

Onboard, Nicole settled into a window seat with her mom beside her. Her dad took the aisle, burying his nose in one of the in-flight magazines. Nicole sighed, attempting to corral her wildly racing thoughts. She stared out the window, watching as the ground dropped away beneath them. The Greek coast was visible below, dotted with islands. Would the plane fly over their island? Would she even recognize it from the air?

"So, you and Fiona, huh?" her mom said once they'd reached cruising altitude.

Nicole turned, unsure what to make of her mother's words. "What about us?"

"Well, you're...together, if I'm not mistaken?"

Okaaaay, maybe her mom hadn't been as clueless when she walked in on Nicole and Fiona in bed together as she'd thought. "Um."

"I think she's great," her mom said. "Is she going to come for a visit?"

"Mom, you just asked me if I'm in a relationship with a woman, and now you're inviting her for a visit before we've even talked about this?" Nicole's brain had flipped on its head so many times since she woke up that morning, she was starting to get whiplash.

"I've always known you liked both men and women. This isn't a surprise." At Nicole's incredulous look, she raised her eyebrows. "I'm your mother. I know these things."

"How?"

"Let's start with the *X-Files* poster in your bedroom in high school, the one where you drew little hearts around Scully's face?"

Nicole's cheeks were on fire. They were really having this conversation right now? On an airplane of all places? "Those hearts were so small, no one could see them but me!"

Her mother gave her a look.

"What were you doing in my bedroom to be that close to the poster?"

"Changing your sheets," her mother said. "And then there was Lauren, in college."

"You knew about Lauren?" Nicole's voice rose.

"You talked about her differently from your other friends. It was obvious you were involved romantically. But you never said anything to me, so I figured I'd let you tell me in your own time, and then you met Brandon, so I didn't see any point in bringing it up."

"Well then." Nicole crossed her arms over her chest. "Does Dad know?"

"I'm sitting right here," her father said pointedly.

"Oh my God." Nicole looked away, pretending a sudden fascination with the puffy clouds drifting outside the window.

"You didn't think we would be disappointed, did you?" he asked.

"No, well...I don't know. We're Catholic." She darted a glance over at him.

"Well, I guess we're the kind of modern Catholics who support our daughter's right to love whoever she chooses."

Tears flooded Nicole's eyes. God, she was an emotional mess this morning. She turned her face toward the window again, blowing out a breath. "Thank you. That means a lot."

"How did you leave things with Fiona?" her mom asked.

"She told me to go home and get my shit together. Sorry." She'd just told her parents she was bisexual, and now she'd graduated to swearing in front of them. Then again, she was thirty-five years old and swore on a regular basis without thinking twice, just not necessarily in front of her parents.

But her mom was laughing. "It was obvious that you two

were smitten with each other. She couldn't take her eyes off you."

"She's pretty determined to keep us apart, actually. She's kind of a recluse in her real life, I think."

"I could see that about her," her mom said. "She looked like she wanted to escape our company a few times, but she was always perfectly polite."

"She wouldn't agree to see me again. She wants me to date other people."

"Are you going to?"

"I don't know. I don't want to, but she has a point. I jumped straight out of my marriage into being stranded with her. Can I really trust my feelings right now?"

Her mom reached over and gave her hand a squeeze. "Then you go home and sort yourself out like she asked you to, and then you fight like hell for her."

13

Fiona wandered her house in a daze. Everything was exactly as she'd left it, and yet nothing was the same. She went into the garden to meditate, but her body felt off-center, as if she was trying to lean on someone who wasn't there. Or maybe it was that she'd left a part of herself behind. She'd spent an inordinate amount of time thinking about the things she and Nicole had left on the island, namely their clothes.

Would someone come along someday and find their dresses hanging from a crumbling column in the pavilion? Would they wonder what had become of the women who'd worn them? These were the idle details that tended to occupy her mind.

Eventually, she settled in her studio overlooking the garden, blank canvas in front of her and a palette of paint to her left. She'd create something to remember their time on the island, something that captured the beauty of what they'd shared, something that might help her regain her balance now that she was home. Exhilaration rushed through her veins at the prospect.

She dipped her brush into the paint and lifted it to the canvas with purpose. *This.* This was what she'd missed while she was stranded on that island. She'd missed the freedom to paint. To create these scenes that manifested in her head, immortalize them in startling color.

Three hours later, she sat staring at the image of their dresses—one red and one gray—fluttering against the ruined Greek columns, but it brought her no joy. It was wrong, the wrong image. Frustration swept through her as she stood, swiping her hands furiously through the paint, smearing it across the canvas until only a streaky mess remained.

At its center, the color merged into a mottled brown, almost like the color of Nicole's eyes or the way her hair looked when it billowed behind her on the ocean breeze.

Fiona had told her to go home and sort herself out, knowing full well Nicole would find someone new in the process, someone steady and dependable, someone who'd take her out for dinner and dancing in all the hottest spots in New York, someone who could offer her everything Fiona couldn't. She'd let Nicole go, knowing she wouldn't come back.

And now Fiona had to make her peace with it, because this was the life she'd chosen for herself, the life she *needed.* Nicole's absence would fade in time.

A knock sounded at Fiona's front door, and emotion blew through her like a hurricane, whirling in her mind. No one ever visited her unannounced. Nicole had come to beg for a second chance, and it was terrible and wonderful, and nothing and everything Fiona wanted, and her feet were already rushing toward the door when the knock sounded again, louder this time.

Strong. Brisk.

A man's knock.

She stalled in the foyer, looking down at her paint-streaked hands, ignoring the pang of disappointment in her chest. "*J'arrive*," she called. *I'm coming.*

She stepped into the washroom, noting the flecks of paint on her face and in her hair. Well, there was nothing for it. Quickly, she scrubbed away as much as she could and walked to the front door, pausing for a breath before she opened it.

Two police officers stood on her front step, wearing Greek uniforms. Why were Greek authorities at her home in France? This obviously had to do with what happened on the *Cyprus Star*, and honestly, it was the last thing she wanted to discuss today. She held in a weary sigh.

"*Yassas*," she said, switching gears. *Hello.*

"Ma'am." The officer addressed her in English, and that was just as well, because her knowledge of Greek was extremely limited. "We're here to speak with Ms. Fiona Boone."

"That's me," she said. "Please come in."

"Thank you," the younger officer said as they stepped inside.

"Can I offer you anything?" she asked, stalling. "Tea? Water?"

"No, thank you."

She led the way into the living room and sat, picking at a flake of red paint under her fingernail as they sat at opposite ends of the sofa across from her.

"Do you know a man called Dimitris Aboulos?" the older officer asked in a heavy Greek accent.

Fiona's head jerked up. Why in God's name were they asking about Dimitris? "Yes, I do."

"How do you know him?" the younger officer asked.

"We've been...acquaintances for a number of years."

"He paid for your voyage on the *Cyprus Star*?"

She paused, drawing a breath to keep the irritation out of her tone. "Yes. He was supposed to accompany me, but he was called away on business at the last minute."

"What kind of business?"

Fiona looked between them. What the fuck was this about? They looked very serious, almost as if she'd done something wrong. Or perhaps Dimitris had. "I don't know. He doesn't share details about his work with me."

"But you believed he would be making the trip with you?"

"Yes." She crossed her arms over her chest, noting a smear of black paint on the bodice of her dress. "What's this about?"

"We will ask the questions here, ma'am," the older officer said.

Fiona's confusion had transformed itself now into concern. "Do I need representation for this conversation?"

"We are not here to arrest you. You are under no suspicion as long as you cooperate with our investigation," the younger officer said.

She stared between them, hands clenched in her lap.

"Can you please tell us what you know of Mr. Aboulos's business dealings?"

"Nothing really." She frowned, searching her brain for anything that might explain why these officers were here, questioning her about Dimitris. "He never talked about work when we were together."

"What did you talk about?" the older officer asked, and Fiona schooled her expression, trying to give him the benefit of the doubt when she wanted to scream, *What the fuck do you think we talked about?* "You said you had been acquaintances for many years. You had planned to take a weeklong cruise together. It sounds like you knew him quite well."

"We only spoke casually," she said, refusing to detail her sex life for these two men. "Food, movies, that sort of thing."

"And was your relationship romantic in nature?"

She narrowed her eyes at him. "Yes, although I have no idea what that has to do with anything that happened on the boat. As you know, Dimitris wasn't even there."

"Mr. Aboulos has been arrested in connection with the hijacking of the *Cyprus Star*."

NICOLE SKIMMED the article that had just popped into her newsfeed. Mostly, she'd avoided the media storm surrounding everything that had gone down on the *Cyprus Star*. She and Fiona had been isolated from it while they were lost at sea and had both declined to be interviewed after they made it home. But this article contained news that a man had been arrested as some kind of mastermind to the whole event, alleging that he had ties to organized crime, and okay, *that* freaked Nicole out a little bit.

She copied a link to the article and texted it to Fiona. *Have you seen this?*

They'd talked only sporadically in the week since they left each other in that hotel room in Greece, and only by text. Nicole was missing her like crazy but trying her best to do what Fiona had asked and sort herself out.

Yes, was Fiona's reply.

Can you believe the guy has ties to organized crime? That's crazy.

Did you actually read the fucking article?

Actually, she'd only skimmed it, and now she had the uncomfortable feeling she'd missed something. She toggled to the browser on her phone and scrolled down, eyes roaming over the details.

"...*long-time girlfriend, Fiona Boone, also a guest on the* Cyprus Star *at the time...*"

The phrase jumped out at her, and Nicole's stomach dropped, dragging her with it into the chair behind her desk. She toggled back to the text window, finger hovering momentarily over the green icon next to Fiona's name before she pressed it. It rang, unanswered, until voicemail picked up.

Dammit, Fi, I know you're there, she texted, and then dialed again.

This time, Fiona picked up on the first ring. "Read it properly now, have you?"

Nicole's breath lodged in her throat at the sound of her voice. "Yes."

Fiona sighed, and the weight of it reached all the way across the Atlantic, settling into the mass of worry in Nicole's stomach. "He'd intended me to be part of it. Apparently, my father's become quite wealthy in recent years. Dimitris thought he might get a nice payout for me."

Nicole pressed a hand to her mouth, looking out at the New York skyline beyond her window. Her arms ached to hold Fiona. She couldn't even imagine what she was feeling about this. "I'm so sorry. So he never planned to meet you on the boat?"

"No," Fiona said tartly. "He lured me onto the *Cyprus Star* so he could hold me for ransom."

"Jesus Christ."

"We screwed up his plans, didn't we?"

"I bet he never thought you'd jump off the boat," Nicole said with a smile. "Fi—"

"I don't really want to talk about him, if you don't mind."

"Okay." Nicole had always assumed that at least part of Fiona's fiercely independent streak was a result of being hurt. How would this latest betrayal affect her? "I miss you."

"Don't," Fiona warned, her tone soft.

"I'm not going to get all sappy on the phone, don't worry."

"Dating anyone?" Fiona asked.

So this was how she wanted to play it? Nicole spun in her chair to face the window. "I signed up for one of those online dating sites, but I'm only doing it for you. I'll go on a few dates with women, but I'm not going to sleep with any of them."

"Do your parents know?" Fiona asked, purposefully ignoring the majority of what Nicole had just told her.

"Yes."

"And they're supportive?"

"Yes. Of my sexuality in general, and of my relationship with you." *Let's see her ignore that one…*

Fiona inhaled sharply. "You told them?"

"I didn't have to. They saw it on their own."

"Very astute of them," Fiona said, tension radiating over the line.

"They like you, and they even like that you're forcing me to figure my shit out before I can see you again."

"Well then."

Nicole squeezed the phone, wishing she could squeeze the human on the other end of the line. "How are you?"

"Fully recovered, although I'm told I'll have a nasty scar."

"I think it will be a beautiful scar."

"It's possible you're biased," Fiona said, but her tone had softened again.

"Oh, I'm definitely biased."

"How's work?" Fiona asked, again steering the conversation away from herself.

Nicole looked around her office, trying to find the right words. "It's the same, but not the same, if that makes any sense."

"Oh." Something in Fiona's voice made Nicole think she might know the feeling. "How so?"

"My job hasn't changed, but I have, if I had to guess." Nicole twirled a pen idly on her desk, watching as the silver clip caught the sun's rays. "I love what I do, and I'm good at it, but my job had completely taken over my life. I was working long hours and hadn't taken a vacation in years. I think...I guess I was partly avoiding having to deal with the fact that my marriage was falling apart."

"You're really taking this self-exploration thing seriously, aren't you?"

Nicole smiled. "I am. Being shipwrecked will do that to a person, I guess."

"Mm."

"So anyway, I've been trying to leave the office on time, spend more time with my friends, that kind of thing. I've got a ton of vacation time stored up, and I'm going to use it, even if I just stay home and read a book."

"You could take up yoga," Fiona suggested.

"Maybe you could teach me."

"I don't teach."

"Not even for me?"

"Especially not you. The ocean between us makes things difficult."

"It doesn't have to."

Fiona was quiet, and the ocean was indeed making things difficult right now, because Nicole couldn't see her to read whether this was a comfortable silence or an uncomfortable one.

Finally, Fiona said, "I have to go."

FIONA WAS AT HER DESK, stylus in hand as she sketched a rough design on her tablet, when her phone rang. Her first instinct was to let it go to voicemail. She rarely answered her phone, hated making idle conversation. Except that tingle in the pit of her stomach reminded her there was someone in the world now she *did* enjoy talking to, someone she couldn't stop thinking about no matter how hard she tried to shut her out of her mind.

So she pressed the button on the stylus and set it down, leaving the outline on her screen half-formed, ten minutes of concentration wasted. She was going to be so pissed if the caller wasn't Nicole.

But it was.

Fiona grabbed her phone, rubbing self-consciously at the huge grin on her face even though no one was here to see it. "Hi."

"Hi," Nicole replied. "How are you?"

"Why do Americans always ask that question?" She stood from her desk and walked toward the back door, stretching as she went.

"Sorry," Nicole said, laughter in her voice. "It's ingrained in us at birth."

"Well, if you really want to know, I'm a bit frustrated with the design I'm working on at the moment, but otherwise fine." She walked into the garden and lay on the chaise by the patio, letting the sun warm her skin.

"Glad to hear it. I went on a date last night."

Fiona's smile withered. "Oh?"

"She was nice. We had dinner at this new dim sum place in Midtown. It was delicious. The mooncakes—"

"She?" Fiona interrupted, trying to sound nonchalant. She closed her eyes against the glare of the sun.

"You insisted that I date," Nicole reminded her.

"Yes, well, I don't recall asking you to phone me up after and tell me about it." And now her mood was ruined, imagining Nicole and her date laughing and flirting over dim sum. That was what she got for answering the phone. She should have let it go to voicemail after all.

"Why, Fiona, are you jealous?" Nicole teased.

"Perhaps," she admitted, deciding there was no point in denying the obvious.

"I called because I wanted to prove a point to myself, and maybe to you too."

"And what's that?"

"That feeling I get when I hear your voice," Nicole said, her tone dropping. "Like a jolt, you know? Right in the pit of my stomach."

"Oh," Fiona breathed as the same sensation rippled through her, like it had when she'd first heard the phone ring, but stronger this time.

"And I didn't feel that with her," Nicole said. "No spark."

"Well, you only just met her."

"I felt it with you the first moment I saw you."

Fiona sucked in a breath, turning her face away from the phone so Nicole wouldn't hear.

"Anyway," Nicole said. "Now that I've proved my point, what are you up to?"

"Working."

"And later?"

"I don't have plans," Fiona said, annoyed and not even sure why.

"I've been keeping busy," Nicole said, undeterred. "Although I'm still resisting my former workaholic ways. I went for a few sessions with a therapist to sort through the divorce, and I even had dinner with Brandon the other night."

"You had dinner with your ex-husband?"

"Yes."

"Why?"

"Closure, I guess? We kind of hashed things out. He seems happy with Claire—she's the woman he left me for."

Fiona rubbed a hand over her brow. "And you're okay with this?"

"I am," Nicole said. "I mean, he fucked up. Big time. But I'm happier now than I was when we were married, so I guess I'm just ready to put it all behind me."

"Mm." Fiona had no idea what to say. Why hadn't Nicole moved on from Fiona the same way she had with Brandon? Or was this call providing her with that closure? It didn't feel like closure, though, at least not to Fiona. It felt like an opening, an opportunity for more.

"Anyway," Nicole said with a sigh, as if she'd just settled into a comfortable chair. Or maybe her bed. "What kind of graphic are you working on?"

"A fucking teddy bear, of all things," Fiona said, feeling a smile tug at her lips.

Nicole giggled. "Why are you drawing a teddy bear?"

"Because that's what I was hired to do. I'll paint something more mature later, to compensate."

"Will you show me, once you're finished?"

"The teddy bear?" Fiona asked.

"Or the painting," Nicole said. "Either. Both."

"Maybe."

"I'll let you get back to it, then," Nicole said with a yawn. "I've got to get ready for work. But I'll be waiting for that text."

"Okay." After she hung up the phone, she sat in the chaise in her garden for a long time, attempting to corral her thoughts, trying not to obsess over what Nicole was doing in her apartment right now or why she'd called, why she kept calling long after Fiona had expected her to lose interest.

Finally, she went back inside and drew the rest of the ridiculous pink teddy bear that the local children's boutique had hired her to create for their new website. And then, before she could change her mind, she took a screenshot and sent it to Nicole.

14

I miss your face. Send me a picture?

Nicole sent the text, holding her breath as the little dots on the screen began to bounce. It had been two months since they returned from Greece, and they'd settled into a routine of texts and occasional phone calls, although Fiona always balked at anything romantic and had so far refused to extend an invitation to France or acknowledge Nicole's open invitation to visit her in New York.

So Nicole was expecting a coy response, some excuse to deflect her request. Instead, she got...

You first.

Her heart leaped, and a giddy grin covered her face. Challenge accepted. She rolled over in bed, surveying her tank top and plaid pajama shorts. Her hair was kind of a mess, but Fiona had certainly seen it worse, and there was no way she was letting this opportunity pass her by. She lifted her phone overhead and snapped a photo, squinting at it. Was it sexy or just silly?

She pushed Send.

God, you're adorable.

Nicole pressed her face against the pillow, still grinning like an idiot. *Adorable's not exactly what I was going for.*

The little dots started jumping again, and this time, an image popped up. Fiona was in bed wearing a silky blue tank top that dipped ridiculously low into her cleavage. Her hair was a mess of curls against the pillow, eyes narrowed behind black-rimmed glasses, and Nicole's whole body went haywire at the sight. Her heart sped, and heat rolled over her skin as if she'd just stepped outside into bright sunshine.

Glasses? she typed.

That's what you get for texting me at 4 a.m. I don't have my contacts in.

Nicole slapped a hand to her forehead. *I forgot the time difference. I'm so sorry!*

It's all right. I was still awake, or I wouldn't have answered.

Why are you up at 4 a.m. looking like that? Should I be jealous?

Don't be ridiculous. I was in my studio, painting.

Nicole scrolled the text box so she could look at the photo of Fiona again. God, she was gorgeous. And sexy. And Nicole wanted her so badly she could hardly breathe. *I've gone on dates. I've spent two whole months here alone in my new apartment, sorting things out, and all I can think about is you. We can take it as slow as you want, be as casual or long distance or whatever you want, but please let me see you again, Fi. I can't stand another minute of pretending you're not the person I want to be with.*

The silence that loomed in the wake of her text was deafening. No dots bounced. Tears spilled over Nicole's cheeks, and she cursed herself for laying it all out there like that. If friendship was all Fiona would let her have, she'd have to find a way to be okay with it, because no matter what, she couldn't lose her entirely.

Dots bounced, and Nicole hardly dared breathe.

Come, then. France is lovely this time of year.

FIONA PACED the designated spot in the airport where passengers greeted the people waiting here to meet them. Her heart was trying to force its way out of her chest, and she simply couldn't stand still, no matter how hard she tried.

It was infuriating. And embarrassing. And miserable.

And then Nicole was walking toward her, and their arms were around each other, and they were kissing, right here in the middle of the airport for the whole world to see. Nicole's kiss was a homecoming, a sensory memory so vivid that Fiona's brain was flooded with images of them together on the deck of the *Cyprus Star*, timid and yearning, huddled on the lifeboat, terrified and wanting, lying beneath the crumbling columns of an ancient civilization, naked and satisfied.

Fiona's heart tripped over itself, and tears stung her eyes. She wound her fingers into Nicole's top, holding on to her tighter than she could ever remember holding on to anything in her whole life. She'd let her go, and Nicole had come back, and Fiona had no idea what to do or think, could hardly breathe past the emotions clogging her throat.

Nicole drew back after a long moment, smiling so widely, her eyes crinkled. "Hi."

"Hi." Fiona gave her one last squeeze before dropping her arms, missing the contact immediately.

"You look good," Nicole said, still smiling. "Different. Even more gorgeous than I remembered."

Fiona gave her shoulder a playful nudge. Nicole's hair

was straight again. She looked different too. And ridiculously beautiful. "Makeup and real clothes and all that. We're not used to seeing each other this way."

"It's just so good to see you." Nicole grabbed her in another hug, arms tight around her, face pressed against Fiona's neck, and she was hugging her right back, unable to pretend she wasn't as affected by their reunion as Nicole was. "You smell good."

"Mm, so do you." Fiona closed her eyes and breathed her in.

"Like sunshine and wildflowers, like what I imagine the French countryside smells like."

"Would you like to see if you're right?"

"Later." Nicole pressed a kiss against her cheek before pulling away. "Right now, I just want to see your house."

"Gladly." Fiona was prepared to be a proper hostess and show Nicole anything and everything she wanted to see while she was here in France, even if all she really wanted to do was take her home and keep her there. So she definitely wasn't going to argue if Nicole wanted to go straight to her house too. Fiona glanced down at the little rolling suitcase beside her. "Do you have other bags?"

"Only this one."

"Let's get out of here, then." She threaded her fingers through Nicole's as she led the way out of the airport. Outside, the sun shone brightly, and a light breeze stirred, tossing Fiona's curls over her shoulders. "I'm parked over here."

Nicole followed her to her little red Fiat. She stowed her suitcase and opened the passenger door. As Fiona sat in the driver's seat, she couldn't stop stealing glances at Nicole. She had on jeans and a flowy pink top with a silver necklace that dipped into her cleavage, and the sight of her was like a shot of adrenaline buzzing through Fiona's veins.

"Do you live near the beach?" Nicole asked as they pulled onto the road leading out of the airport.

"I'm afraid not."

"That's okay." Humor laced Nicole's voice. "I'd say we've already done the beach. But maybe we should visit while I'm here, just for old time's sake."

"Dip our toes in the surf?" Fiona darted another glance and found Nicole watching her intently.

"Mm-hmm."

It was all Fiona could do to keep her hands on the steering wheel and her eyes on the road until they'd made it to her house. Usually, the drive relaxed her, all the lush green hills and pastures. Today, she was driven to distraction by the woman beside her.

"It's so beautiful," Nicole said as they turned onto Fiona's street. "The houses are so adorable. No wonder you love it here. You must want to paint everything you see."

"I do." Fiona glanced over at Nicole again. She wanted to paint her most of all. At last, her cottage came into view, and she turned into the drive, rolling down the dirt path to her garden.

"I love it already," Nicole said as she climbed out of the car. "It's so...you."

"Well, I should hope so. I live here." Fiona gave her a hand lifting her suitcase out of the boot before leading the way inside. They went in through the door into the kitchen, and almost immediately, Nicole was in her arms again.

"I missed you so much," she murmured between kisses, her hands in Fiona's hair, bodies pressed together, skin touching everywhere, and Fiona felt her world shift into alignment for the first time since she'd come home from Greece.

She slid her hands up to cup Nicole's face, brushing away the tears that dampened her lashes as she kissed her breathless. When they finally came up for air, Nicole's nipples had hardened beneath the thin material of her top.

Fiona trailed her fingers down Nicole's chest to the silver pendant she wore around her neck. "Pretty."

"A gift from one of my friends. It's supposed to be good luck."

"Pity you weren't wearing it that night on the boat."

"She gave it to me after I got home."

"Friend, hm?" Fiona couldn't help the note of jealousy that had entered her tone.

"I don't kiss any of my other friends, Fi," Nicole said, tightening her arms around her.

"Are we friends?" Fiona asked. She didn't have many of those. Acquaintances, mostly. People she'd meet in town for a cup of tea and then not talk to for another month. Nothing like her obsessive need to see and talk to Nicole every moment of every day.

"Friends. Girlfriends. Both, I hope." Nicole brushed her lips against Fiona's. "I didn't kiss any of my dates either, just so you know."

"No?" Fiona felt an odd sort of relief at the news, although she was the one who'd insisted Nicole date. "I haven't either...kissed anyone. Or gone on a date, for that matter."

"Such an adorable hermit." Nicole cupped her cheek, eyes warm and teasing.

"Do you want anything? Are you hungry?" Fiona had gone shopping earlier to fulfill her role as hostess, hoping Nicole wouldn't mind staying in.

"Only for you," Nicole answered. "It's been a long, lonely couple of months." Her hands slipped beneath Fiona's top, sweeping around to palm her breasts.

"Tell me about it." Fiona arched into her touch, and they were kissing again, hands groping, clothes flying everywhere as Fiona guided her toward the bedroom. They just barely made it, falling naked onto the bed, and there were so many things Fiona wanted to do with her now that they had the time and opportunity to do them, but Nicole had her pinned to the bed, kissing her way down her body, and Fiona couldn't think past the pleasure of her touch.

"So pretty," Nicole said, twirling Fiona's belly ring. "It matches your eyes."

Fiona had chosen it because it reminded her of the ocean at their island, had wondered if Nicole would comment on it, but hadn't expected her to compare it to her eyes.

"And this," Nicole continued, sliding lower, "is the most beautiful scar I've ever seen."

"Is it?" Fiona asked, squirming slightly, aroused to the point of distraction.

Nicole's fingers traced the reddened area below Fiona's right knee, and she shivered. "Does it hurt?"

"No," she whispered. "Just sensitive."

"I'm so glad to have you whole and healthy."

"And able to get on my knees?" Fiona joked, her fingers twining in Nicole's hair.

Nicole laughed. She pressed a kiss against the scar before settling between Fiona's thighs, and she was already halfway gone on anticipation alone. Nicole stroked her first, her fingers sliding over Fiona's sensitive flesh, and she exhaled deeply, eyes closed, surrendering herself to the sensation of being touched and the pleasure Nicole could bring.

"You always do that," Nicole murmured.

"Do what?" she gasped, because she was having a hard time forming words right now.

"Sigh like that when I first touch you." Nicole stroked her again. "Like you've been waiting for it forever."

"It feels like I have."

"You don't have to wait anymore." Nicole's tongue pressed against her clit, and Fiona arched off the bed. She wondered briefly how Nicole could be so good at something she'd only done once before, and then she was pulled under the growing tide of pleasure inside her, gasping and writhing, hips moving against Nicole's tongue as she worked her magic.

Fiona closed her eyes and held on for the ride. Nicole licked, sucked, and plunged, eventually focusing the attention of her mouth over Fiona's clit while she pushed two fingers inside her.

"Yes," Fiona moaned as everything inside her tightened.

Nicole repeated the action once, twice, and Fiona shattered, release flowing through her in blissful waves, obliterating everything from her mind but peace and pleasure and the overwhelming beauty of this thing she shared with Nicole.

"You are really fucking good at that," she whispered, drawing Nicole up against her. Their bodies slid together like two halves of a whole, and Fiona had no idea how she was supposed to let her go again at the end of the week.

15

Nicole lingered in the doorway as Fiona walked ahead of her into the studio, wanting to observe her for a moment in this room that must be her favorite, her oasis, her creative place. She walked to the easel and turned to face Nicole, a dreamy smile on her face.

This was what Nicole had come to France hoping to find: this version of Fiona. The Fiona that stood before her now in a long, flowing green dress, eyes gleaming with health and peace and happiness.

"There's something I wanted to show you," she said.

"Did you paint me?" Nicole asked teasingly, stepping into the studio. It was a sort of all-weather porch at the rear of the cottage with windows on three sides to let in lots of natural light and a large wooden easel in the center. A tarp covered the floor, spattered with paint every shade of the rainbow.

"Sort of," Fiona said, gesturing to a painting on the wall beside the door.

Nicole turned to face it, pressing a hand over her mouth. It was them—her and Fiona—or a fantasy version of them.

They wore the red strips of fabric they'd fashioned out of Fiona's dress on the island, hands entwined as they dove deep below the turquoise waves of the ocean.

"I call it 'Fire Under Water,'" Fiona said, coming to stand beside her.

"It's...it's beautiful, Fi."

"I tried painting us on the island, but I could never get it quite right."

"This is perfect," Nicole said, staring mesmerized at the painting. "I love it."

"I'm glad." Fiona's fingers slid into hers, squeezing gently.

"I keep that drawing you made for me beside my bed."

"Do you?"

Nicole nodded. "It helped me feel close to you, when I was there, and you were here."

"I guess I felt the same way about this one." Fiona leaned in, resting her head on Nicole's shoulder the way she'd done that endless night on the lifeboat when everything had been so terrifying and miserable.

"I'm so glad I'm here."

"Me too."

They stood there for a long minute, holding each other and staring at the painting of them diving together in a turquoise sea in their flaming red outfits. *Fire under water*. If that didn't describe everything they'd been through...

"Do you want to go out, or...?" Fiona asked.

"Not tonight. I mean, unless you want to." But she already knew Fiona didn't, and tonight, she was the only thing Nicole wanted.

"No," Fiona said. "You must be tired from your flight."

"I am." And she really wanted to keep Fiona all to herself tonight. But sooner or later, they needed to try their relationship out in the real world. So far, they'd existed together mostly in a void. They'd never gone on a date or even gone shopping. And before she went home, Nicole wanted to see at least a little bit of the French countryside.

Instead, they got domestic together. Chatting comfortably in Fiona's kitchen, they prepared a chicken to roast with various root vegetables and a handful of fresh herbs Fiona had bought that morning at the market. This was something Nicole rarely did. Sure, she'd cooked plenty of meals for Brandon over the years, but from scratch was hardly her forte, and with them both working full-time in the city, they'd often resorted to takeout or pre-prepared meals.

Since the divorce, Nicole was more likely to fix herself a sandwich and eat on the couch in front of the TV than make a home-cooked meal. Cooking with Fiona was oddly comforting, though. Once the food was in the oven, Fiona poured two glasses of wine, and they sat on the back patio, watching the sun settle below the trees.

"I see why you love it here so much," Nicole said softly.

"It's peaceful."

"A world away from New York."

"City mouse meets country mouse," Fiona said with a smile.

This was the part Nicole wasn't sure how to resolve, and ironically, geography ought to have been the least of their problems. But if Fiona gave her the chance, Nicole would embrace a long-distance relationship, and maybe eventually, it could be more. Maybe they could split their time together between New York and France.

Over the past few weeks, Nicole had been considering the possibility of leaving her corporate life behind. She could open her own marketing firm and work from home.

She had the experience to make it work. Now that she was here, sitting in Fiona's garden sipping wine, body humming from the magic they'd shared in bed and her heart fuller than it had been in years, she felt like the future was hers for the taking, as long as Fiona was a part of it.

"You're awfully quiet over there," Fiona said with that amused look on her face, the one Nicole had seen so often during their journey together.

"Just thinking how much I like it here."

"Do you like the wine?"

"Yeah, it's nice." Nicole took another sip. "Wait a minute…"

Fiona's eyes sparkled. "Remember it now?"

"You bought the same wine we drank on the boat?"

"I already owned it, actually. Told you it was a good one."

"Well, cheers." Nicole leaned over, tapping her glass against Fiona's. "To the wine that led to our first kiss." She had so many questions about what had happened after that first kiss. About the man, Dimitris. And Fiona's father. What had happened that day in the hospital room? Fiona hadn't said a word about it after he'd left.

But Nicole wasn't going to ask them tonight. Tonight was for everything warm and wonderful, and she meant to enjoy every moment.

"WHAT DO your neighbors think of you?"

Fiona turned at the unusual question, narrowing her eyes at Nicole. "How do you mean?"

"I mean, are you the nice neighbor who buys groceries for the old lady down the street or the kooky artist who keeps to herself and people whisper about when they see her leave her house?" Nicole smiled. She was joking, but her words still hit a bit of a sore spot.

"Somewhere in the middle, I suppose."

This was Nicole's third day in France, and Fiona had brought her into the heart of Nice to the touristy area she generally avoided. They'd shopped together, had dinner at an outdoor café, and were now strolling along the seaside, shopping bags in hand.

"Today's been so amazing," Nicole said, a relaxed smile on her face.

"It has," Fiona agreed. Sometimes she spent so much time avoiding people, she forgot she didn't mind being around them from time to time, and especially with Nicole at her side.

"I think we have to do it," Nicole said, looking at her like they were about to rob a bank together.

"Do what?" Fiona had no idea what she was getting at.

"Put our toes in the ocean."

The way she said it, so earnest but with that wicked smile, Fiona turned to kiss her but instead found herself doubled over in laughter. She laughed until tears leaked from her eyes, and then she took Nicole's hand and dragged her toward the beach. They dropped their shopping bags in the sand, kicked off their shoes, and jumped in.

With waves lapping at their knees and half the population of Nice turning to stare, Fiona wrapped her arms around Nicole and kissed her deeply and thoroughly.

"Well, that was nice," Nicole said when they'd come up for air.

"Wasn't it?" Fiona nudged her nose against Nicole's and gave her another quick kiss before leading the way back to the pavement. Her dress was wet below the knees, her toes gritty with sand, but she didn't care. They'd drawn quite a crowd, though, and that she did care about...just a little.

She'd become something of a local curiosity after Dimitris was arrested. Between the notoriety of having been lost at sea and her connection to the man behind it, for a little while, everyone had been looking at her. And so, she found she didn't like it now. She wanted to be just another nameless face in the crowd, a woman out for a walk with her girlfriend.

She hustled Nicole back to the car a bit more quickly than she probably should have, claiming her wet clothes bothered her. Nicole wasn't fooled, having spent a week in wet clothes with Fiona, during which neither of them had spent much time complaining about it, but she played along, talking cheerily about their day as Fiona drove them home.

"Did it bother you, all those people watching us kiss?" she asked finally as they walked into the cottage.

"No...I mean, I don't mind kissing you in public. Everyone who knows me knows I date women." She walked to the kitchen and poured wine, handing a glass to Nicole.

"Then what?" she persisted, and Fiona smiled softly, wondering that she'd ever thought she might have gotten off from this line of questioning.

"There's just been a lot of staring since everything that's happened. Those weren't random onlookers. They recognized us, or at least some of them did. People are curious. And I don't like being stared at for reasons that are none of anyone's business."

"Oh." Nicole sat at the table, sipping her wine. "Tell me, Fi. Tell me what wasn't in that article. What really happened with Dimitris?"

Fiona sighed, settling into the chair beside her. "I was naïve, that's what happened. I was a fool."

"You're anything but a fool," Nicole said, reaching for her hand.

"This time, I was. I met Dimitris about five years ago. I'd been invited to a gallery event where a few of my paintings were on display. He was there. We hit it off. He was rich and charming, but not in the pompous way men often are. He was enjoyable to be around, and he was good in bed. He traveled a lot on business, which brought him to Nice once or twice a year, and we fell into a routine where he'd phone me up when he was in town, and we'd spend a day together, maybe a couple of days, if I wasn't seeing anyone else at the time, which, let's face it, I usually was not."

Nicole opened her mouth as if she had questions, then closed it and gestured for Fiona to continue.

"I never looked him up. Frankly, I wasn't interested enough in him to care, but that was my mistake, because if I'd searched his name, apparently I would have found that he'd been questioned by the police multiple times over the years for his connection to organized crime." She paused, sipped, looked over at Nicole, sipped again. "So when he asked me on this cruise with him, I thought it sounded like fun. Like I said, I was a fool."

"If that's foolish, then I'm an idiot too, because I've never run a Google search on anyone I've dated, including you. You're human, Fi. You made an error in judgment."

"What happened to your marriage?" Fiona asked, turning the tables on her.

It was Nicole's turn to sigh, to settle into her chair for a tale she'd rather not tell. "We married young. We were so much in love back then. It's hard to remember now, but we were. But then we grew up, our careers grew up, and before we knew it, we were two strangers sharing a house, fighting over stupid shit and resenting each other for being the people we'd become. And eventually, he found someone else."

"Growing apart isn't an excuse to cheat," Fiona said quietly.

"No, it's not, and I can't forgive what he did, but I've moved on. I don't hate him. We weren't happy for a long time before he cheated, and that wasn't anyone's fault. It just was. One of us should have had the courage to walk away years ago."

"Always easier to see in hindsight." Fiona swirled her wine, staring into its ruby-red depths.

"It is. But it made the divorce easier, in a way. I wasn't in love with him anymore, so the feelings weren't as raw. Emotionally, I'd been alone so much longer than three months. And having been in a loveless marriage, it makes me appreciate even more when things are good." She leaned forward and kissed Fiona, a kiss that made what they'd shared on the beach in Nice look like a peck on the lips, the kind of kiss that sent clothes flying and ended in bed.

They rolled together over the sheets, hands roaming, hips rocking, mouths never losing contact in their desperate tumble toward release. Nicole broke first, hips jerking against Fiona's as she came with a cry that brought Fiona right over the edge with her. They ended in a tangled heap of body parts, breathless and sweaty, giddy smiles on their faces. Fiona's heart felt so light, she could hardly stand it. This was the effect Nicole had on her. It was strange and terrifying and wonderful, all at the same time.

Exhausted, they drifted off to sleep in each other's arms. When Fiona woke, it was dark outside, but she couldn't see the clock without disturbing Nicole, so she snuggled closer against her, mentally replaying a highlight reel of their day, and there were a lot of highlights.

"Are you awake?" Nicole whispered.

"Yes."

"We're so lucky, aren't we? To have escaped that ship and survived everything we did on the lifeboat and the island, and to have found each other in the process." Nicole's arms tightened around her, her voice rusty with sleep and edged in nostalgia.

"Lucky is one word for it."

"You don't think so?"

"Lucky isn't usually a word I use to describe myself, no." She heard the bitterness that had slipped into her tone, immediately hating it, but she couldn't change the truth either.

"Why is that?" Nicole asked, her question whispered into the dark, echoing endlessly inside Fiona's brain. "What happened with your family? With your dad?"

It was a question that reminded her of a time in her life when she'd slept with her bedroom door locked and a flashlight under the covers. She felt herself stiffen at the memory, knowing Nicole felt it too but helpless to prevent it from happening.

Nicole squeezed her gently, moving one hand to stroke her face. "What did he do to you?" she asked, her voice quiet but fierce.

Fiona looked away, even though it didn't matter in the darkness of her bedroom. "It's not so much what he did as what he didn't do."

"What didn't he do?" she whispered. "Who did he not protect you from?"

Air whooshed from Fiona's lungs, her chest collapsing like a ruptured balloon. She pressed a hand against it, willing herself to find air, to form the answer to Nicole's question, but neither came. Her lungs burned, and her vision blurred, and tears splashed over her cheeks.

Nicole brushed them away with a touch that was heartbreakingly gentle. "You don't have to tell me if it's too difficult."

Her lips brushed Fiona's, and that contact seemed to break something inside her, the dam holding her emotions in check. She buried her face on Nicole's shoulder and cried, big racking sobs that shook her entire body, leaving her weak and shaky, a limp and soggy version of herself who was tired of drowning in her own private sorrow.

"It was my Uncle Timothy," she whispered against Nicole's skin, wet with Fiona's tears.

"Oh, dammit," Nicole breathed, her arms holding Fiona against her, holding her together. "I'm so sorry."

"He didn't visit often, but when he did…" She squeezed her eyes shut, trying to block out the memories. The pain, the shame, the bruises she'd had to wear tights under her skirts even in the summertime to hide.

Nicole's hand stroked her hair in the dark, giving her the strength to continue.

"He went away for a while, and the next time he came to stay with us, I was old enough to know what was happening. I told my mother. She screamed and cried and locked herself in her bedroom. My father swore a lot and couldn't look at me. I thought he didn't believe me."

"Oh no," Nicole whispered.

"After I went to bed that night, I heard the yelling, my father and Uncle Timothy. He said he would call the police if his brother ever set foot in our house again. The next morning, my uncle was gone."

"He should have called the police anyway." Nicole's voice

was filled with quiet outrage. "Did your uncle ever face charges?"

"No." Fiona cleared her throat, hoping it might add some strength to her voice. "Maybe he would have, but he went home and killed himself instead."

"Oh my God." Nicole's arms tightened around her.

"It was awful," she whispered. "So much fucking crying. My mother never stopped. My father never left his study. I never left my room."

"Oh, Fi... Didn't anyone hug you?"

She laughed bitterly. "The Boones weren't very prone to hugging."

"I may have to hug you forever to make up for it," Nicole whispered.

Fiona drew strength from Nicole's embrace to finish the story. "A few weeks later, my mother died of a heart attack."

"Oh my God. Oh, Fiona..." Nicole pressed their foreheads together, cupping Fiona's face in her hands. "That's... that's maybe the saddest story I've ever heard."

Fiona sucked in a deep breath, inhaling the scent of Nicole's hair.

"How old were you?"

"Twelve."

"And what happened? It was just you and your dad left?"

"He told me after my mother's funeral that he had failed us. I didn't think he had. Not yet, anyway. But he retreated into his work after that. We hardly ever spoke. That's when he failed me. The housekeeper looked after me, mostly. I was angry. So fucking angry." She breathed again, holding onto Nicole in the darkness.

"I'm angry *for* you," Nicole said fiercely. "And so sorry."

"I was a nightmare teenager," Fiona said. "I skipped curfew and drank too much and tried too many drugs and slept with too many people. I yelled at my father when he tried to discipline me. I just wanted someone to hear me, and he never fucking did."

"He should have, dammit. How did you get from there to here?"

"I grew up, despite my best efforts otherwise. My father paid for me to get my degree in graphic arts, again despite my best efforts otherwise. I moved out. I got a job I hated, and eventually, I came here."

Nicole kissed her, holding on to her in the dark, her anchor, her center, her *everything*. "What happened when he came to visit you in the hospital in Greece?"

"I think...I think he wanted to talk, but I couldn't, not then. I shut him out, so in the end, he just said he was glad I was okay. Like I've ever been *okay*." Fresh tears slid over her cheeks.

"You're more than okay," Nicole said. "You're a survivor. You're smart and strong and successful and one of the most amazing people I've ever met."

"Don't." She buried her face against Nicole's shoulder.

"It's the truth."

"I can't believe you're here." In her life, in her bed, in her heart. Any or all of the above.

"Believe it," Nicole whispered. "And I'm not going anywhere."

Nicole woke to an empty bed. Not a surprise. She'd woken alone every morning since coming to stay with Fiona, almost every morning since they'd met. But this morning, she hoped Fiona wasn't regretting her middle-of-the-night confession. Nicole didn't know how to adequately express how much she appreciated Fiona sharing it with her or how fucking sorry she was for everything she'd been through. She could only keep on loving her the best way she knew how and hope it was enough.

To that end, she went into the bathroom to freshen up and then went in search of Fiona. She found her in the garden—on her head.

"That's just not humanly possible," she said with an affectionate smile.

"Amateur," Fiona said without opening her eyes. She did these yoga poses on her mat in the garden...these really crazy yoga poses that involved contorting her body into positions that Nicole would never attempt in a million years.

"Want me to make tea?"

"Please."

Their morning tradition. Relief loosened in Nicole's chest. Somewhere during the night, she'd become convinced Fiona would freak out and push her away, the defense mechanism of a woman accustomed to wrangling her demons alone.

But it wasn't happening. And now Nicole found herself wishing and hoping that this would bring them closer together, that Fiona would allow her to be the person who broke through her barriers, maybe the person who became a permanent part of her life.

Because Nicole was helplessly in love with her, and she knew Fiona loved her too. Whether she'd ever admit it or act on it was a different question entirely.

They had breakfast together on the back patio—toast and grapes with English breakfast tea. Nicole was starting to get used to the European way of life. Fiona looked like a goddess in her low-waisted yoga pants and sports bra, jewel glinting from her belly ring and matching glitter on her toes.

"It's unfair for anyone to look that good in workout clothes," Nicole said.

Fiona slid an amused look in her direction. "You should give it a try sometime."

"What—yoga? I have. I don't look like you when I do it. I'm not graceful...like, at all."

"It takes practice."

"Well, maybe sooner or later, you'll help me find my grace, then," Nicole told her.

Fiona looked away, and maybe Nicole was still worrying for nothing, but suddenly, it felt like the air between them had chilled.

"We should paint something together," Nicole blurted as they were cleaning up breakfast.

"What?"

"Teach me. It could be fun." She was envisioning them in the studio together, paintbrushes in hand, laughing and splattering each other with splashes of color as they created some kind of messy masterpiece together.

"Perhaps."

"Unless you had something else in mind for us to do today?" Nicole asked.

Fiona shook her head, leading the way into the studio. "What do you want to paint?"

"Anything. I don't care. What do you suggest?"

Fiona was silent a moment. "The ocean seems appropriate, doesn't it?"

"Yes," Nicole answered without hesitation. It was so obvious, she couldn't believe she hadn't thought of it herself.

Fiona hauled out a blank canvas and placed it on the easel, her body distractingly lithe in her yoga clothes. "The first thing you want to do is sketch out your vision."

"Like, waves?"

"The horizon, the shoreline, any landmarks you want to include," Fiona said.

"I think we should paint the middle of the sea, the way it looked when we were bobbing in the lifeboat, just waves everywhere."

Fiona planted her hands on her hips. "That's actually harder. It's difficult to make the ocean stand out without something to contrast it against."

"Well, I'm not trying to win any awards here, just have fun. But what if we include our lifeboat in it?"

Fiona nodded, looking pleased. "I like that."

"You sketch it. I'll help paint," Nicole said, both because she sucked at drawing and because she wanted an excuse to observe Fiona at work. She leaned against a stool and watched as Fiona took a pencil to the canvas. "Wait, you're a leftie?"

Fiona's eyebrows rose. "You're just noticing?"

"I haven't watched you work before, and yes, I'm just noticing. Never mind. Carry on."

Fiona lifted her left hand and sketched an outline of their lifeboat toward the right-hand side of the canvas. Then she added a faint line Nicole presumed would be the horizon about a third of the way down the canvas. She turned to Nicole. "Next, we need paint...and smocks. And even so, I'd recommend changing if you're particularly attached to those clothes."

Yeah, Nicole had noticed that most of Fiona's casual things had paint spots on them. She looked down at her jean shorts and tank top. "I don't mind if these get messy."

Fiona took two paint-spattered smocks from a rack in the corner. She tossed one to Nicole and tied the other around her own waist. Nicole watched as she took out a white plastic tray and began to pour small dollops of paint onto it. She added several different shades of blue, purple, green, black, and finally white.

"Those are a lot more colors than I thought we would use," Nicole said, coming to stand beside her.

"There's a lot more color that goes into painting than you realize," Fiona said. She dabbed a brush into one of the lighter blue paints and demonstrated a few strokes for Nicole. "We start like this, and we'll layer in more depth of color as we go."

Nicole selected a medium-sized brush and dabbed it into the same light blue paint Fiona had started with. A wide smile broke on her face as she swiped her brush against the canvas, creating a rich band of color. This was fun. Painting together had been a good idea. They worked side by side, leaning over each other, occasionally swapping brushes and paints.

Fiona demonstrated various techniques to add depth and texture to the waves. She squirted yellow and orange onto their palette and added the sun shining in the sky above. She outlined their lifeboat in vivid orange and showed Nicole how to reflect the color in the waves around it. They spent most of the day in the studio together, taking periodic breaks for food and rest.

Fiona seemed relaxed and at ease as they worked, occasionally pausing to kiss Nicole or touch her, shoulders and hips bumping as they smeared oil onto canvas.

"It's a masterpiece," Nicole announced when the painting was finished. In truth, it had turned out much better than she'd expected, and that fact was due in large to Fiona's ability to shape Nicole's hapless brush strokes into something beautiful. Their orange lifeboat floated on a rolling sea, waves stretching across the canvas as the sun beat down from above.

"I love it," Fiona agreed, her fingers squeezing Nicole's. She turned toward her, untying the smock from behind her back. Nicole lifted it over her head as Fiona untied her own smock. She hung them both on the rack in the corner.

"You've got a little something." Nicole swiped at a dot of blue paint on Fiona's nose, smearing it.

"You do too." Fiona touched a spot on Nicole's cheek.

"Made it worse," Nicole said with a grin, rubbing at the paint smear on Fiona's nose.

They stared at each other for a moment. Fiona's eyes sparkled mischievously, and then they moved almost as one, reaching for the palette still sitting by the easel, paints blended here and there from the colors they'd mixed for their painting.

Fiona dipped a finger into the sea of blue and smeared it across Nicole's cheek, grinning wickedly. Nicole swiped her finger through the orange and traced a line of it down Fiona's chest, swirling it around her belly ring like the sun peeping over the horizon of her blue pants.

It was all downhill from there. They painted each other, kissing and touching, hips moving, seeking contact, colors mixing, blending, their desire illustrated in vivid hues.

Fiona tugged at the button of Nicole's shorts, looking at her paint-colored hands. "Shower," she whispered.

Following her train of thought, Nicole nodded eagerly. They tumbled into the shower together, shedding clothes against the white tiles. Fiona soaped up her hands, scrubbing away paint. Nicole followed her lead. They kissed as the shower beat down on them, washing each other and teasing by equal turns. Fiona pressed Nicole against the tiles, sending rivulets of blue-tinged suds down her chest and over her nipples.

"Now this is a masterpiece," she said as she used her hands to sluice hot water over Nicole's skin, chasing it with her mouth. She dragged her teeth along the underside of Nicole's breast before swirling her tongue over her nipple, and Nicole let her head clunk against the tile.

"Your mouth..." she managed, hands sinking into the wet depths of Fiona's hair.

"You like it?" she asked, peering up at Nicole through a wayward curl.

"I love it."

"More than just my accent?" she asked, batting her eyelashes as her tongue continued to explore Nicole's breasts.

"I love that too." Nicole gasped as Fiona slid a hand

between her legs, stroking her as she continued to use her deliciously talented mouth on Nicole's breasts.

"I'll keep that in mind," she said, sounding so overbearingly British that Nicole almost called her on it, but it turned into a moan as Fiona dropped to her knees, bringing her beautifully British mouth against the most intimate parts of Nicole and rendering her unable to speak.

She braced herself against the tile, straining to hold herself upright as Fiona worked her magic, shattering Nicole into a million blissful pieces as easily as she'd created beauty on the canvas in her studio. They rinsed off, dried off, and tumbled into her bed, where Nicole returned the favor.

"This has been the most amazing day," Fiona said as they lay together afterward, sounding relaxed and at peace with the world. Their toes bumped beneath the sheets, foreheads pressed together, hands clasped between their bodies.

Nicole wanted to hold onto this moment, bottle it up, and keep it with her forever.

OVER THE NEXT FEW DAYS, they made even more perfect moments. They toured an art museum, a winery, and a castle. They bought food and flowers at the market and spent a quiet evening at home, sipping wine and sharing stories. They made another painting together, this time of the flower arrangement they'd gotten at the market, but the lifeboat remained Nicole's favorite. Fiona even attempted to show her a few yoga moves in the garden.

There were glimpses—little moments tucked between bigger ones—when Nicole thought she saw Fiona pulling back, distancing herself, perhaps preparing for an ending much bigger than Nicole's upcoming return to New York. It was there in the way she paused, paintbrush in hand, her eyes a million miles away when Nicole mentioned a phone call from her parents, the way she turned her back when Nicole lamented having to be at work on Monday.

Maybe she was just being paranoid. But there was no way she was going to let Fiona shut her out, not after everything they'd shared this week. On Saturday night, Nicole's last night in France, they went out to dinner at a local brasserie and spent the rest of the evening in bed, making the most of their final hours together.

Nicole rolled over, resting an arm over Fiona's waist. "I don't want to go home tomorrow."

"Don't think about it yet," Fiona whispered.

"Will you come?" Nicole asked.

Fiona gave her a coy look, purposely misunderstanding her. "I'm capable of doing that by myself, you know."

"To New York, you pervert." Nicole shifted her hand, toying with Fiona's belly ring. "Will you visit me?"

"I hate cities," Fiona said, turning her face toward the ceiling.

"I'll take you to the countryside, to the mountains, anywhere you want to go."

Fiona was silent, staring up at the ceiling fan that slowly swirled the air around them, spreading the scent of the fields outside, grass and wildflowers and livestock mixed with a lingering scent of paint from the studio behind them.

"Don't do this," Nicole said as tears stung her eyes. "Don't push me away, not now."

"I'm not," Fiona said, her voice as faint as the birds chattering outside.

"Then tell me we'll see each other again. Let's plan it. Right now. Get your laptop, and let's book our next trip."

A tear slipped from Fiona's eye, disappearing into her hair.

"Come on, Fi. All I'm asking for is the chance to see you again."

"We'll see."

And everything Nicole had feared hung plainly in Fiona's words, in her voice, in the vacant stare in her eyes. "'We'll see' is a cop-out. It's an excuse to send me home so you can shut yourself away from the inconvenient fact that I've come along and made you care about me despite your best effort not to."

Fiona sucked in a harsh breath, jaw set, eyes fixed on the ceiling.

Nicole curled herself around her, unwilling to be shut out, not this time. "And I care about you too. The best part of my day—every day since we got home from Greece—has been you. Whether it's a text or a phone call or just staring at the sketch you made for me, you make me happy, Fi. I want to be with you. I love you."

Fiona tensed beneath her, more tears sliding over her cheeks, disappearing into her hairline. She closed her eyes. "You don't mean that."

"I do. I love you more than I've ever loved anyone. I love watching you do ridiculous yoga poses on your head. I love lying next to you in bed...and all the other things we do in it. I even love eating food cubes with you. Do you realize how happy we were on that island? It should have sucked, and a lot of it did, but honestly, there isn't another person on earth I'd rather have been stranded with."

"Stop it." Fiona finally softened, rolling toward her. Her eyes blinked open, staring into Nicole's, the color in them as vivid as the paint they'd used to create the ocean in her studio.

"I love your eyes," Nicole whispered. "They're like our beach...turquoise and gold where the water meets the sand."

"It's hereditary," Fiona said softly. "The gold ring. My mother had it too."

"I love you, Fi. And I know you're not ready to say it back yet. Just say we'll see each other again after I fly home tomorrow."

"You're barely out of your marriage," Fiona said, her voice gone deep and husky the way it was when she was emotional. "You've never even been with another woman."

Nicole sighed, running her fingers through the honeyed depths of Fiona's hair. "I know how I feel."

"I don't know how—" Fiona pressed her lips together, eyes glossy.

I don't know how to love you back.

Nicole was almost certain that was what Fiona had been about to say, and the knowledge ripped her apart even as it broke her heart. "This isn't about me or my divorce, not anymore. You know that, right?"

Fiona was silent, her bottom lip quivering slightly.

"Dammit, Fi, you told me to go home and find myself, and I did, but you didn't do the same. You're still lost, and you're too afraid to admit it."

Fiona squeezed her eyes shut, hands clenched into the sheet between them.

Not knowing what else to say, Nicole rolled away, facing the door. She sucked in breath after breath, trying to keep her emotions in check, until finally, she surrendered and let the tears flow.

"I'm sorry," Fiona whispered from behind her.

"Yeah, me too."

They lay like that for what felt like hours, backs to each

other, lost in their own misery. The tension between them festered like an open wound, and this one couldn't be so easily healed with a round of IV antibiotics. This one required words and actions that Fiona might not ever be ready to say or take.

Eventually, Nicole drifted into a troubled sleep. Sometime during the night, instinct took over, and she woke to find herself wrapped in Fiona's arms, her chest wet with Fiona's tears.

She'll come around. She will.

But when Nicole woke the next morning, the bed was empty. Even though this was a totally normal part of their routine, Nicole's stomach turned to lead. This felt different somehow, after the way they'd left things last night. She slid out of bed and walked to the back door. The garden was empty. The driveway was empty.

Fiona was gone.

Nicole's throat closed up. Her vision went hazy, and she bent over to stem the buzzing in her ears. Furious, she marched back into the house and picked up her phone. Sure enough, Fiona's name glinted on the screen.

I called a car to take you to the airport. I still hate goodbyes.

And then...

I'm sorry.

With shaking fingers, Nicole typed back, *Fuck you.*

No dots bounced. No reply came.

This time, Fiona wasn't coming back.

17

Fiona stared at the mess in her bed, unsure whether to laugh or cry. Nicole had dumped the entire pot of turquoise paint on her sheets. Fiona knew she was an unforgiveable bitch for leaving this morning, but she hadn't been able to face the reality of letting Nicole go, and now she had to own the consequence.

She sat on the edge of her bed, swirling her fingers through the paint, trying to fight the sinking sensation inside her, like she was a black hole being sucked cell by cell into the gaping void in her chest.

Her gaze sharpened. There, next to her pillow, finger painted in vivid turquoise, were the words, *I love you.*

And then she started to cry. She curled in the middle of her paint-soaked bed and cried until she was a miserable, shuddering mess. Why was she like this? Sometimes she thought she must be irrevocably broken inside, rendered incapable of love after too many years spent without it.

Here she was alone...again. Nicole's words echoed endlessly inside her head.

You're still lost, and you're too afraid to admit it.

The first part of Nicole's statement was definitely true. She was lost. So fucking lost. And okay, fine, she'd been too scared last night to admit it. The problem was, she couldn't be found, not nearly as easily as Nicole had gone home and gotten herself together.

Fiona was just...like this. And people like her weren't suited to relationships. She'd always known it. She'd been happy alone, preferred it that way, even. When Nicole first came into her life, she'd thought it might turn out to be a good thing. They could be friends, see each other occasionally, screw each other's brains out when the opportunity presented.

But love her? Fiona didn't know how to do that, was certain she'd fuck it up. So she'd taken the easy way out. Or at least it had felt like the easy way a few hours ago. Now, instead of standing at the airport kissing Nicole goodbye, she was alone in a bed full of paint.

With a heavy sigh, she sat up, annoyed with herself for getting it all over her clothes and in her hair, annoyed with Nicole for pouring paint in her bed. By now, it had probably soaked into the mattress, and that was a hell of an expensive thing to replace. She climbed to her feet and slid the top sheet off the bed, but instead of crumpling it up, she folded it so the words *I love you* faced up and set it in the corner of her room.

She'd throw it away...later.

She stripped away the rest of her bedding, confused when she found one of the drop cloths from the studio in the mix. And then she held back a laugh, because even furious and jilted and heartbroken, Nicole had put a tarp under Fiona's sheet before she poured paint on it. She'd protected the mattress.

Fiona slid the whole mess into the hamper to deal with

later. She stripped out of her paint-stained clothes and took a shower. And then she attempted to get on with her day, her week, her life.

She created a halfway decent graphic for one of her clients and sat for a long time in her studio, staring at a blank canvas. In her early morning fit, Nicole had also taken their painting—the one of the lifeboat bobbing in the ocean —and thrown it facedown on the floor. Fiona couldn't bring herself to pick it up. So it lay there, an echo of every failure that had befallen her since she'd set foot on the *Cyprus Star*.

She'd been a fool to think a man would buy her voyage on a vessel like that without expecting something in return. She'd been a fool to let herself fall so deeply for Nicole. She'd been a fool to invite her here, to give them both a taste of how it could have been when she'd always known she would never be able to make it work.

Enough foolishness. She gathered her bag and headed to the market to find something for supper. At least that was something she could do like a normal person. She didn't have the heart or the energy to cook today, though, so she selected a container of premade soup and brought it to the counter.

The employee there—a woman named Manon who rang up Fiona's purchases almost every day—gave her a shrewd look, a smile curling the corners of her mouth. "I almost didn't recognize you in those clothes," she said in French.

Fiona looked down at herself. She had on black trousers and a gray top, nothing outlandish. "Why is that?"

"I'm used to seeing you in something much more..." She paused for a moment as if searching for the right word. "Colorful."

"Oh." Well then.

Fiona tucked her chin, paid for her soup, and headed home.

The next few days passed in painful monotony. She did her morning yoga. She meditated—even if she still felt slightly off-balance without Nicole as her focal point. She met her deadlines and even painted something new. Unfortunately, it turned out as gray and depressing as her mood. It would appear that Nicole had sucked all the color right out of her house when she walked out the door.

I love you.

The finger-painted message taunted her from the corner of her bedroom, but she couldn't bring herself to throw the ruined sheet away. Not yet.

Even the calendar had begun to taunt her. As August rolled into September, she was forced to face the date looming ahead. On the tenth, she would turn forty. It was no big deal. Age was just a number. She hadn't felt much about it one way or another as the date approached, but now that it was nearly here, she couldn't help wondering—what did she have to show for the first forty years of her life?

And the answer was: not a hell of a lot. She lived alone, had few friends, was estranged from her only living family member, and had pushed away the only person in recent years brave enough to love her.

The only person in recent years Fiona had been brave enough to love back.

She didn't want to turn forty alone. She didn't want to be alone for another fucking second. Her cottage was so empty these days, it was about to swallow her whole.

She picked up her phone and scrolled backward through her texts from Nicole, all the way back to the night they'd exchanged selfies in bed. The night Fiona had agreed to let her visit. She looked at the photo of Nicole in her ridiculously adorable pajamas, hazel eyes crinkled in one of her irresistible smiles, the kind of smile that made Fiona feel worthy of being looked at that way. When she was with Nicole, the world felt lighter and brighter. The plain truth was, Fiona didn't want a life without her. And maybe their love was worth the risk of her fucking it up.

Because maybe, if she got out of her own head and just let Nicole love her, she wouldn't fuck it up. Maybe it was that easy. No, it wouldn't be easy. It would be one of the hardest things she had ever done, but it might also be the best, certainly the most important. Nicole had gone home and sorted herself out when Fiona asked her to. Now it was time for Fiona to do the same thing.

I have so many regrets, her father had said.

God knew Fiona had regrets, a lifetime of them, but right now, not letting him explain himself that day in the hospital ranked near the top. What would he have said?

She remembered the cards he'd sent over the years, the times he'd called—calls she'd never returned. He'd closed himself off from her as a child when he felt like he'd failed her, pushed her away out of fear, the same way she'd done to Nicole. The same way she'd been pushing him away throughout her adulthood.

Maybe he'd come to her hospital room to make things right. Maybe it was time to let him. And maybe it was time for her to do the same.

Choking on the terror clogging her throat, she closed out of her messaging app and booked herself a flight to London. She packed a bag. And she made the long flight home.

The following morning, she stepped out of a taxi in front of the granite-fronted row house where her father lived now. Sucking in the biggest breath she'd ever taken in her life, she walked up the front steps and lifted the knocker.

Her whole life seemed to flash before her eyes as she waited, listening for the sound of his footsteps. The creak of her bedroom door when Uncle Timothy pushed it open. The horror and revulsion in her father's eyes when she'd told him the truth. The bitterly cold rain that fell on her shoulders as she stood over her mother's grave.

The door swung open, and her father stood there, looking impossibly old and gray. His eyes widened, his fingertips white where he gripped the edge of the door.

"Dad," she managed, clinging desperately to her composure.

"Fiona."

For a moment that seemed to last an eternity, they just stared at each other. Her heart beat so fast, her ears buzzed, her stomach a hard knot lodged somewhere beneath her rib cage. And then her rigid, impassive father pulled her against his chest, arms shaking as they encircled her, tears streaming down his face.

"I'm so sorry, sweetheart. So very sorry."

18

When Nicole first got back to New York, she'd checked her phone about a million times, hoping against hope that Fiona might call or text. Apologize. Explain. Ply her with some pathetic attempt to stay friends that Nicole would have to decide if she was strong enough to accept because the thought of losing her entirely was unbearable.

But the days passed, and nothing came. No call. No text. Nothing. And Nicole was forced to accept that their relationship was irrevocably, completely over.

It was the loneliest week of her life, even though she was surrounded by people for the majority of it. She got up and went to work every day. She went out with her friends for girls' night. She went to her parents' house for a home-cooked meal and some much-needed affection, courtesy of her mom, a game of chess, courtesy of her dad, and a much-needed smile, courtesy of her younger brother, Michael, who came to dinner with his brand-new fiancée.

None of them could ease the emptiness in her heart. How must it feel to be Fiona, all alone in that cottage in the

French countryside? Was she missing Nicole even half as much as Nicole missed her? The most heartbreaking part of the whole scenario was that Nicole suspected the answer was yes.

When September tenth rolled around, Nicole holed up in her apartment, wondering what Fiona was doing to celebrate the milestone. Was she at home with a glass of wine? Out with friends? A man? A woman?

The thought turned Nicole's stomach, but no, she didn't think Fiona would have moved on yet. Probably, she was home alone with a glass of wine. That was how she'd told Nicole she wanted to spend her birthday, after all. Alone. Eternally alone.

Oh, Fi...

Idly, Nicole picked up the sketch Fiona had left in their hotel room in Greece. She'd drawn them in bed together, bodies entwined, hair a mixture of light and dark across the pillows.

But the table beside the bed...

Nicole shrugged up on her elbows and turned on the lamp to get a better look. She'd seen that table, and not in their hotel room. It was the table beside Fiona's bed in her cottage in France. Those were the sheets Nicole had poured paint on. She recognized the zigzagged stitching along the seam. This was Fiona's bedroom. And, now that she was really looking, the thin line below Fiona's knee wasn't a wound but a scar.

She'd drawn a future version of them, at her home, healthy and healed and cuddled in bed together. What did that mean? Was it an apology or a promise?

And the question that had been lingering in the back of Nicole's mind all day suddenly loomed to the front—should she call Fiona on her birthday? Maybe send her a text?

What time was it in France right now? Late. Probably too late to call. She looked at the clock. It was past eight here, which meant it was already well past midnight in France. Her birthday was over. Fiona was forty, and they were both still alone.

Nicole rolled facedown in bed, fighting back tears.

Someone knocked on her door, and she lurched upright. Aw, dammit, here she was in her pajamas with red-rimmed eyes, and she was going to have to face down a neighbor or well-meaning friend who'd decided to drop by unannounced.

The thought briefly crossed her mind to ignore the knock, roll over in bed, and pretend to already be asleep. At eight fifteen and with all her lights on? Yeah, right.

With a sigh, she climbed to her feet, checked her appearance in the mirror to make sure she was at least basically presentable, and shuffled to the door. Without bothering to check the peephole, she pulled it open, and then she reeled backward in surprise.

"Hi," Fiona said, staring at her out of eyes even more tired and red rimmed than Nicole's. She wore black pants and a formfitting black top, her hair pulled back in a messy ponytail so that her dark roots all but hid the golden depths of her curls, a duffel bag slung over her shoulders, and she couldn't have looked any less like herself if she'd shown up in a ball gown and glass slippers.

Nicole just gaped at her for a long minute, unable to believe Fiona was actually on her doorstep, looking like this dim, glum version of herself.

"I, um, I hope you hadn't rescinded my invitation to visit?" Fiona said, going for a joke, but her voice cracked about halfway through. Her eyes welled with tears, and...*dammit*.

Nicole wrapped her arms around her, squeezing her tight. "I'm still furious with you," she whispered through her own tears. "Don't forget that just because I'm also ridiculously glad to see you."

"May I come in?" Fiona asked with a tight smile, swiping a palm over her cheeks.

Nicole gestured her inside, closing the door behind her. "Did you really fly all the way to your least favorite city in the world on your birthday?"

"I did." Fiona twisted her fingers, her eyes darting around the apartment before landing on Nicole's.

"Why?" she asked, because her heart was swelling with all kinds of possibilities, and they were almost all good. She couldn't take it if Fiona was here for any other reason.

Fiona blew out a breath. "I did what you told me to do," she said finally, her voice small.

"What was that?" She hardly dared hope...

"I went home," Fiona said, and okay, *that* wasn't what Nicole had expected.

"Home?"

"To see my father," she said quietly. "I've been in London most of the week."

"Oh my God." Nicole couldn't help herself, she was hugging Fiona again, dragging her toward the couch. She set her bag on the floor, and they sat, side by side. "How did it go?"

"Okay," Fiona said with a quick nod. "We talked quite a bit. He apologized...so did I."

"Fi, that's so good. Oh, I'm so glad."

"Yeah, me too." She took Nicole's hand in hers, her grip surprisingly strong. "I think I found the thing I was hiding from. We faced our demons, my father and I."

"That's really great." Her words felt painfully inadequate, but she didn't know how to tell Fiona just how glad she was that she'd finally been able to make peace with her past.

"We still have a lot of healing to do. *I* have a lot of healing to do. But I'm willing to do it." Fiona turned toward her, eyes wide and vivid, swimming like the Mediterranean, an emotional hurricane churning in their depths. "I don't want to be alone anymore."

"Oh, Fi..." Tears splashed over Nicole's cheeks, and her heart felt like it was wringing itself inside out.

"So I came here to this awful city on my fucking birthday to tell you I love you," Fiona said, the words tumbling out of her, chest heaving, fingers clutching Nicole's. "I'm sorry for running out on you like I did. I was scared and stupid, and I promise..." She drew in a ragged breath. "I'll try to do better next time if you'll give me the chance."

And then they were kissing, tears mingling on their faces, arms wrapped so tightly around each other Nicole could hardly breathe.

"Of course," she gasped. "Of course, I'll give you the chance. I love you, Fi, so much."

"I've been miserable without you," Fiona said, kissing the tears from Nicole's cheeks. "It's been fucking awful."

"Same," Nicole said, laughing through her tears. "Let's not do that again, okay?"

"Never." A smile broke over Fiona's face, her lips red from their kisses, cheeks flushed a happy pink, eyes impossibly blue, color coming out from behind the storm clouds that had obscured her when she first came to the door.

"I have the craziest urge to get on my knees right now and propose to you," Nicole whispered.

"Oh God." Fiona slapped a hand over her mouth.

"I'm not going to, at least not today. You're not ready.

Hell, *I'm* not ready. But just know that I plan to love and cherish you for as long as we both shall live, regardless, okay?"

Fiona nodded, crying in earnest now.

Nicole leaned in, pressing her nose against Fiona's cheek. "You crossed an ocean for me today."

Fiona turned her head, bringing their lips together. "And I'd do it again."

They kissed, deep and drunk and desperate, weeks of pent-up longing bursting into flames between them.

"You're the first person I've ever felt this way about," Fiona whispered into their kiss. "I've thought about you every moment since we left Greece, even when I thought I'd never see you again. It took me forty years to fall in love, to find someone I could imagine spending the rest of my life with. It's safe to say you're it for me."

Nicole grinned at her, wiping the tears from Fiona's cheeks. "I knew you were a romantic at heart."

"Only for you," she whispered, pulling Nicole in for another kiss.

"Oh, and Fi?"

"Yes?"

"Happy birthday."

EPILOGUE

ONE YEAR LATER

"I can't believe I let you talk me into this."

Fiona glanced over her shoulder at Nicole. "You love me."

"You're insane." Nicole huffed as she picked her way over the scrubby ground toward the crumbled marble pavilion ahead.

"In a good way, I hope?"

"That remains to be seen." But she was smiling, and Fiona took that as a yes.

"This time, there's a boat just offshore waiting to whisk us back to the mainland the moment we're ready to leave." Fiona stepped into the pavilion, spinning to take it in. Nothing had changed since they'd raced into the darkness that fateful night, chasing after a distant Greek fishing boat. Their dresses—one red and one gray—fluttered from the pillar where Nicole had hung them after their last washing, tattered and faded now like ancient artifacts.

"I can't believe they're still here," Nicole said, tracing her fingers over the ragged edge of Fiona's red dress.

"I always wondered if they would be."

"Do you think someone will visit this island years from now and wonder what happened to the women who left them behind?" Nicole asked softly.

"The thought did cross my mind." Fiona sat at the front of the pavilion, facing the ocean, legs dangling, much as she'd sat that night when she was too sick to sleep. Today, she wore a dress the color of the ocean beckoning below. It whipped around her knees in the sea breeze.

Nicole sat beside her, khaki capris brushing against Fiona's bare leg. "Okay, maybe it wasn't totally insane to come here on your birthday. It's kind of...romantic."

"I hoped you'd think so." Fiona looked over at her.

Nicole's hair blew in the breeze, her hazel eyes warm as the sun overhead. So beautiful she took Fiona's breath away every time she looked at her. Somehow, this amazing woman had seen past all her bullshit to fall in love with her.

In the past year, they'd started their own business together—Athena Marketing, so named in honor of this very place. Nicole had left the corporate world to work from home. She offered a range of marketing solutions for her clients, including branding packages, with Fiona creating the logos and graphics. Finally, she had a job she didn't hate, a job that left her plenty of time—and inspiration—to paint, a job that let her spend all her days with Nicole.

They split their time between her cottage in France and the new house Nicole had bought in New Jersey, near her parents. Fiona's "Fire Under Water" painting hung proudly in their living room, while Nicole's finger-painted "I love you" was framed above their bed in France. She had given up her New York City apartment on one condition: that she and Fiona book a fancy hotel room there several times a year and spend the weekend. They'd done it four times so far, and Fiona hadn't hated a single minute. Even the city was bearable when she had Nicole to share it with.

It hadn't all been smooth sailing. Fiona had spent a lot of time—too many hours to count—in therapy, sorting through all her shit. She and Nicole visited her father in London, and while it had begun awkwardly, the end result was a sense of peace and contentment Fiona had never known possible.

"Forty's been great," she said, "but I hope forty-one will be even better."

"How could it not be?" Nicole leaned in to place a kiss on her lips.

"There's just one more thing I want for my birthday."

"More than coming here?" Nicole's eyebrows went up. "Unless it's something I can give you back at the hotel, because..."

Her voice drifted away to nothing as Fiona reached into the pocket of her dress and pulled out two rings set with aquamarine the color of the Mediterranean lapping at the beach below.

"Marry me?" Fiona said, twirling them on her index finger. "Here. Right now."

Nicole pressed a hand to her mouth, tears welling in her eyes. "I can't! My family would kill me."

"We'll have a legal wedding in the States for them, but let's do this here just for us...for me," she added, because Nicole probably wanted a big wedding as much as her family did, but all Fiona really wanted was this moment here in the spot where they'd first made love, where they'd fallen in love, and now, hopefully, where they'd seal their love with a ring and a promise.

"Yes," Nicole whispered, tears spilling over her lashes.

Fiona handed her one of the rings. They faced each

other, Greek columns behind them, the Mediterranean below, memories whipping in the sea breeze.

"Nicole Morella, you have made this the best, happiest year of my life. I didn't think I'd ever have anything like this." She swiped at the tears on her face. "I think I fell in love with you the first moment I laid eyes on you in that bar on the *Cyprus Star*. You're just...everything I never knew I wanted or needed to make my heart full."

"And you, Fiona Boone, are the woman who gave me the courage to embrace myself for who I am, to take a leap even when things are scary as hell. You helped me see all the colorful, wonderful things I was missing, and I've never been happier since you took me out on that deck and kissed me."

"I love you," Fiona whispered, sliding her ring onto Nicole's finger.

"Love you too." Nicole repeated the gesture, and then they looked down at their hands, matching rings glinting in the sun.

"I never in a million years thought I'd get married, but if I'd ever imagined my dream wedding, this would be it." Fiona leaned in to kiss her bride. "Just you and me and nature as our witness."

"It's perfect," Nicole said, kissing her back. "Absolutely perfect."

They lay back on the marble together, hands entwined. Fiona closed her eyes, feeling Nicole's warm presence beside her. Her wife. They'd been lost in paradise here together, but Fiona had still been lost even after she'd returned to France. She'd found herself in Nicole's embrace, her kiss, her strength, and now, for the first time in her life, Fiona had finally found her way home.

ACKNOWLEDGMENTS

Thanks as always to my family for being so supportive. I know this job doesn't always make it easy! Thank you to my editor, Linda Ingmanson, for your expertise and to my amazing critique partner, Annie Rains, for always guiding me in the right direction.

Stranded books are some of my favorite to write, but they also involve the most research. Thank you to Will Goodwin for your medical expertise and to Victoria Denault for helping out with a few words in French.

A huge thank you to all the readers, bloggers, and reviewers who've read my books and supported me along the way. Love you all!

xoxo

Rachel

Keep reading for a look at the first chapter of my next book, *Don't Cry for Me*!

A frosty television host, a bubbly bar owner, and a litter of abandoned kittens. The recipe for ratings gold...or heartbreak?

DON'T CRY FOR ME

CHAPTER ONE

Eve Marlow's heels clicked confidently against the polished floor as she strode down the hall toward her producer's office. She paused outside the door, running her fingers over the front of her dress to smooth any wrinkles before lifting her hand to knock.

"Come in," Greta called from inside.

Eve grasped the handle and pulled the door open. Greta sat behind her desk, glasses perched on her nose as she looked up from her computer screen. But she wasn't alone. Bruce Koslowski, *Life & Leisure*'s director of advertising, stood beside her. "Greta," Eve said with a polite smile. "Bruce, this is a surprise."

"Hello, Eve," Bruce said with an equally polite nod.

"Have a seat." Greta gestured vaguely to the guest chairs in front of her desk.

Eve sat, placing her laptop on the edge of the desk.

"I'm afraid I have some bad news," Bruce said.

Eve nodded. "Greta told me this morning that the ratings for our season two premiere weren't as high as we'd hoped, but I've put together several proposed adjustments to *Do Over*'s advertising plan that I think should—"

"Actually, that's not why I'm here," Bruce interrupted. "You can discuss advertising with Greta later."

More bad news? Eve straightened in her seat, clasping her hands loosely in front of herself. "All right."

"We have to pull episode eight," Bruce said.

"The ice cream shop?" Eve said, incensed. "That's one of our strongest episodes. Why on earth would we scrap it?"

His lips drew into a frown. "The owner has been charged in a sexual assault."

Fuck. Eve felt a heavy sensation in her stomach, as if the remnants of her lunch had hardened into concrete. "That's...not good."

"I know," Greta agreed. "It's a publicity nightmare. There's no way we can air it."

"Is there time to shoot a replacement?" As the CEO of Marlow Marketing, Eve had built an empire helping underperforming small businesses reach their potential. Two years ago, the *Life & Leisure* channel had offered her a television show—*Do Over*—that followed her as she worked. Each episode featured a different business, offering viewers the chance to become invested in their success as she helped them rebuild. Season one had been a runaway success. So far, season two was off to a lackluster start, and without this episode, she might be in real trouble.

"It's possible," Greta said. "But the timing would be extremely tight."

Bruce's frown deepened. "I'm afraid there's no room in the production budget to reshoot, even if you were able to fit it into the schedule."

"I'll make room in the budget," Eve said automatically. This was what she did for a living, after all. She saved failing businesses, and now she would save her television show, because if she didn't get her ratings up, *Do Over* would never get renewed for a third season. "I'll draw up a revised advertising plan."

"If you're able to make room in the budget, I'll think about it, but I'm not making any promises," Bruce told her. "Have it on my desk by the end of the day."

She nodded. "Consider it done."

Bruce left, and Eve slumped in her chair. "How much time do I have to find a new client and shoot a replacement episode?"

"Not much," Greta told her apologetically. "You'd need to bring me the client's name by Friday, with filming to begin next week."

Eve pressed her knuckles against the edge of the desk in front of her, letting the cold wood bite into her skin, providing an outlet for her frustration. "Friday, as in the day after tomorrow?"

"Yes. And first, you've got to make room in the budget and have Bruce sign off on it," Greta reminded her.

"I'll do that right now." Eve stood, picking up her laptop.

Greta nodded, waving a hand in Eve's direction. "Go work your magic. You'll pull this off. I have full confidence in you."

"I will," Eve confirmed. She left Greta's office and strode down the hall toward her own. They had hundreds of leftover applications from their season two casting call. The trick would be finding someone who could bring her the ratings she needed, when she'd already chosen what she'd believed to be the ten strongest applicants from the bunch. Hopefully, she'd overlooked a potential breakout star.

First things first. She closed the door to her office and spent the next two hours reallocating funds from *Do Over's* already stretched advertising budget to allow her to shoot the replacement episode. As much as she needed those advertising dollars, she needed a full season more. She emailed the revised budget to Bruce and settled in to sift through previously rejected season two applications.

But as the sun slid behind the Manhattan skyline outside her window, she was no closer to finding a replacement client and her stomach had begun to growl obnoxiously. Stifling a growl of her own, she packed up to head home. She'd find something to eat, change into her pajamas, and keep working.

Preferably with a glass of wine.

Since it was going to be a late night, she stopped in the break room to fix herself a coffee for the ride home. She spent her thirty-minute subway ride making notes on her phone, outlining ways to maximize what remained of her advertising budget. While Marlow Marketing wasn't in any trouble, *Do Over* was dangerously close to cancellation. She enjoyed filming the show. It had become an important part of her brand, and perhaps most importantly, it had tripled her income. She wasn't going to lose it, not when she knew it could be saved.

Her cell phone rang as she exited the subway, and Greta's name showed on the screen. Eve connected the call. "Please tell me you're calling with good news."

"I am, actually," Greta told her. "They've signed off on your revised production budget. All you have to do now is bring us a new client in time to get the replacement episode filmed."

"Excellent." Eve exhaled in relief as she dodged a bike messenger, stepping aside to let him pass. "I'll let you know as soon as I have a name."

"Friday," Greta reminded her.

"Got it." Eve tossed her empty coffee cup into a nearby trash can. A tiny, muffled cry echoed from somewhere, and she paused. "Did you hear that?"

"Hear what?" Greta asked.

"Nothing. Listen, I'll check in with an update tomorrow morning, okay?" She strode down the street toward her building, intent on getting upstairs, out of these heels, and warming up something for dinner. Where had that cry come from? Had it been something on Greta's end of the line? It hadn't sounded human, more like an animal. Probably someone nearby on the street was watching a video on their phone or carrying some kind of exotic pet. This was New York City, after all. She'd once seen a man carrying a tiny pig in a backpack.

But an uneasy feeling deep in her gut worried that the sound had come from inside the trash can, and it only grew stronger with each step she took. Holding in a sigh, she turned and walked back to the bin. It was filled almost to the top with garbage. Eve couldn't believe she was even contemplating poking around in a public trash can. God knew what was inside, but it was sure to be disgusting.

She grimaced as she stood there, listening. Other than the steady hum and honk of traffic, laughter from a couple passing by, and the distant roar of a jet overhead, she couldn't hear a thing. She was being ridiculous. Hours of work awaited her in her apartment, so she had no idea why she was standing here, staring at a trash can. To satisfy her conscience, she turned on the flashlight on her cell phone and shined it inside.

There was her coffee cup, laying on a plastic grocery bag at the top of the garbage pile. No animals. Nothing but gross, smelly trash. She wrinkled her nose, shining the light quickly over the rest of the bin, but...did that bag just twitch?

Oh, hell.

It twitched again. A sick feeling washed over her, all thoughts of ratings and clients wiped from her mind. With her free hand, she reached cautiously into the bin, nudging aside her coffee cup to uncover the bag beneath it. She hesitated before touching it. What if the movement was caused by a rat, rooting through the rubbish? Or something even less friendly?

But that stubbornly uneasy feeling in her gut made her grasp the knot where the bag had been tied shut and lift it out of the bin. Something inside squealed, and Eve's heart slammed into her ribs. Her skin prickled. Oh God, there was really a live animal trapped inside this bag. What kind of sick joke...

She knelt and placed the bag on the ground. Cautiously, she tore a hole in the plastic, keeping her fingers well away from the opening in case whatever was inside tried to bite her. She'd just free the rat and be on her way. But the tiny creatures inside weren't rats. The bag was full of some kind of baby animals that looked like...were those kittens? Tiny newborn kittens, eyes closed and barely moving.

Eve exhaled harshly, as if the wind had been knocked out of her. She ripped the bag all the way open and reached inside. Her fingers brushed soft black fur, and the kitten mewled softly, rooting its head toward her hand. It was cool to the touch.

"Jesus," she murmured, scanning the rest of the animals. She counted six total, a mixture of black, gray, and one solid white kitten. Not all of them were moving. Oh *fuck*. Were they even alive?

She stripped out of her blazer and laid it on the ground.

Carefully, she lifted the kittens out of the bag one by one and placed them inside her jacket, trying not to notice how cold and stiff they felt beneath her fingers. The temperature hadn't quite reached seventy today, average for mid-April in Manhattan. She needed to get them inside and warm, and then...what?

She'd call the animal shelter. Yes, that was the logical next step. She eyed the bag they'd been inside of. Should she take it with her? Was it evidence? Was it a crime to throw a litter of kittens in the trash? She sure as hell hoped so. And so she balled up the empty grocery bag and tucked it inside her blazer, which would be going straight into the wash—if not the trash—once she got home. She scooped the edges of the fabric together, forming a makeshift sack for the kittens, and hurried toward her apartment building.

A cool breeze whipped through the thin material of her blouse, and she shivered. Several people gave her strange looks as she cradled her blazer in front of herself. She resisted the urge to tell them off, reasoning that in their position, she'd give herself an odd look too.

Eve Marlow, up-and-coming reality television star, behaving bizarrely among rumors that Do Over's *second season is off to a disappointing start.*

This day could really just stop now. She'd had enough. Walking briskly, she rounded the corner and approached her building. She'd take the kittens inside, call the shelter, and get them on their way to help and veterinary care. Then she could get back to work.

Morris, the doorman, held the door open for her. "Good evening, Ms. Marlow."

"Evening, Morris. Thank you." She offered him a brief but grateful smile on her way to the elevator. There hadn't been a peep out of the kittens since she'd put them in her blazer. No wriggling. God help her if she was carrying a jacket full of dead kittens up to her apartment right now. What if they were covered in fleas? Or had rabies? Was she endangering herself by bringing them inside?

She punched the button with her elbow and waited, toe tapping impatiently, until the elevator arrived. It carried her swiftly to the eighth floor, and she let herself into her apartment. There, she stood for a moment, unsure what to do next and halfway terrified to look inside her blazer.

But her discomfort was no excuse for further endangering their lives. She lay her blazer on the kitchen table, spreading it flat. A few of the kittens stirred, mewling as they scrambled toward each other for warmth.

Several of them didn't move at all.

She shuddered. They were so cold. Thinking fast, she went into the bedroom, rummaging through her closet until she found the heating pad she used when her back started acting up. She carried it to the kitchen table and plugged it in before laying the jacket full of kittens on top of it. "Now to find someone to take you."

She washed her hands—just in case—then sat at the table and pulled out her phone. She looked up the nearest animal shelter, only to receive an automated recording that it was closed for the night. Same story at the next shelter. And the next. It was only seven o'clock. Wasn't there any place to take abandoned animals after hours? These kittens wouldn't make it until morning. Not to mention, she didn't have time to deal with this, not in general and especially not tonight.

Eve stared at the furry pile of kittens. What the hell was she going to do with them? She'd never had a pet, never cared for an animal in her life. She had no idea how to care for these, but they were obviously too small for solid food.

They probably needed milk. Maybe she could warm up some of the half-and-half she kept in the fridge for her morning coffee, but what would they drink it out of?

They were so small, so helpless.

Irritation warred with concern inside her as she typed "what to do if you find abandoned kittens" into the search bar on her phone. The top result was a YouTube video with the thumbnail of a woman with lavender hair holding a kitten about the size of the ones Eve had found. For lack of a better option, she pressed Play.

"Hi, everyone. It's your favorite kitten rescuer, Josie Swanson, here to tell you what to do if you find an abandoned kitten or litter of kittens," the woman in the video said.

Eve leaned back in her seat as the knot in her stomach loosened. This video might be exactly what she needed. Josie was pretty, with warm eyes and an endless smile. Eve had never been a fan of unnatural hair colors, but the lavender seemed to work for Josie, accentuating her bubbly personality.

Unfortunately for Eve, the video mostly covered how to care for newborn kittens rather than where to take them. But, worst-case scenario, it might help her keep them alive through the night until she could drop them at the shelter in the morning.

"The important thing to remember is to never bring a litter of orphaned kittens to an animal shelter," Josie said, staring earnestly into the camera. "Most shelters aren't staffed to care for bottle-fed babies and will have to euthanize them. The best thing to do is to reach out to local animal rescues and ask for their help. I've included a list of resources in the description below."

Well, this wasn't good news, but that seemed to be the

theme of Eve's day. Then again, maybe she could find an animal rescue that would take the kittens tonight. She scrolled through the links below the video until she found a kitten rescue in New York City. According to the contact information, Josie herself ran it. Maybe Eve's luck had turned. She'd give the kittens to Josie and be done. Josie would know exactly how to care for them. She had over a million subscribers and countless videos detailing all the kittens she'd saved.

Eve clicked on the contact button and composed a quick message detailing her situation, adding URGENT to the subject line, because she wasn't sure these kittens would survive another hour without intervention, let alone overnight. And as much as she needed to get to work and find a client for her replacement episode, she did *not* want a pile of dead kittens in her kitchen...or on her conscience.

Not knowing what else to do, she rewatched Josie's video while she waited. They'd need kitten formula, which she could apparently get at most pet stores. So much for the half-and-half in her fridge. She had just pulled up a list of local pet stores when her phone rang with an unknown Manhattan exchange.

Eve connected the call. "Hello."

"Hi," came the vivacious voice from the video. "This is Josie Swanson. You've found a litter of abandoned kittens?"

"Yes," Eve told her gratefully. "Someone dumped them in a trash can."

"It happens all the time, unfortunately," Josie said. "About how old are they, if you had to guess?"

"Newborn, maybe," Eve said. "Their eyes are still shut, and I think their umbilical cords are still attached. Can I bring them to you tonight? I'm honestly not sure how long they're going to survive otherwise."

"I'm so sorry, but I can't take them. I'd be happy to meet you, show you how to care for them, and give you some supplies, though."

Eve's stomach clenched in a combination of disappointment and frustration. She'd been so sure Josie was going to help her. She was tired and hungry, her feet ached, and she needed these kittens out of her apartment so she could get back to the mountain of work awaiting her. "I don't understand. You run a kitten rescue. Why can't you take them?"

"I really wish I could, but I own a bar in Brooklyn, and we're short-staffed at the moment. I'm tending bar twelve hours a day, and these guys will need round-the-clock care."

Eve bristled at the implication. "I work full-time too. I can't keep them."

"Look, you're in Manhattan, right?" Josie asked.

"Yes."

"Tell you what. Bring them here. I'll make some calls while you're on your way and see if I can find someone to take them for you. If not, I can give you some formula and show you how to care for them, at least temporarily."

"Bring them to your bar?"

"Yes," Josie confirmed. "Sorry, but I'm working all night."

Eve's entire body tensed, and her pulse quickened. She couldn't handle walking into a bar, especially not tonight. Her gaze fell on the kittens. What choice did she have? But if she brought them to Josie's bar, she was going to convince her to keep them, because there was no way Eve was bringing them back home with her. "I'll be there in half an hour."

ALSO BY RACHEL LACEY

Love in the City

Read Between the Lines

Vino and Veritas

Hideaway

Midnight in Manhattan Series

Don't Cry for Me

It's in Her Kiss

Come Away with Me

Almost Royal Series

If the Shoe Fits

Once Upon a Cowboy

Let Your Hair Down

Rock Star Duet

Unwritten

Encore

The Stranded Series

Crash and Burn

Lost in Paradise

The Risking It All Series

Rock with You

Run to You

Crazy for You

Can't Forget You

My Gift is You

The Love to the Rescue Series

Unleashed

For Keeps

Ever After

Only You

ABOUT THE AUTHOR

 Rachel Lacey is an award-winning contemporary romance author and semi-reformed travel junkie. She's been climbed by a monkey on a mountain in Japan, gone scuba diving on the Great Barrier Reef, and camped out overnight in New York City for a chance to be an extra in a movie. These days, the majority of her adventures take place on the pages of the books she writes. She lives in warm and sunny North Carolina with her family and a variety of rescue pets.

facebook.com/RachelLaceyAuthor

twitter.com/rachelslacey

instagram.com/rachelslacey

amazon.com/author/rachellacey

bookbub.com/authors/rachel-lacey

Printed in Great Britain
by Amazon